Why Are Parents So Unfair?

"I can't believe it," Jessica cried. "This is the worst thing that's ever happened to me in my whole life. I just can't believe that Mom and Dad won't let me go to the party, Lizzie. I'll be the only sixth-grader who's not there!"

"I won't be there either, Jess," Elizabeth reminded her twin.

Jessica sank down in the chair. "Well, it's not fair," she said angrily. "Mom and Dad don't trust us. They're treating us like babies because they don't think we've got the sense to take care of ourselves."

Elizabeth sighed. "I don't think it's a matter of trusting *us*," she said. "It's the other kids at the Hangout that they don't trust."

Jessica's eyes flashed. "It's so unfair! They're ruining our lives because of something we didn't do!" She glared at Elizabeth. "They're not my bosses. I'm twelve years old, and they can't tell me what to do!"

D0029253

Bantam Books in the SWEET VALLEY TWINS series
Ask your bookseller for the books you have missed

SWEET VALLEY TWINS

The Twins Get Caught

Written by
Jamie Suzanne

Created by
FRANCINE PASCAL

A BANTAM SKYLARK BOOK®
NEW YORK · TORONTO · LONDON · SYDNEY · AUCKLAND

RL 4, 008-012

THE TWINS GET CAUGHT
A Bantam Skylark Book / September 1990

Sweet Valley High® and Sweet Valley Twins are trademarks of Francine Pascal

Conceived by Francine Pascal

Produced by Daniel Weiss Associates, Inc.
33 West 17th Street
New York, NY 10011

Cover art by James Mathewuse

Skylark Books is a registered trademark of Bantam Books, a division of Bantam Doubleday Dell Publishing Group, Inc.

All rights reserved.
Copyright © 1990 by Francine Pascal.
No part of this book may be reproduced or transmitted in any form or by any means, electronic or mechanical, including photocopying, recording, or by any information storage and retrieval system, without permission in writing from the publisher.
For information address: Bantam Books.

ISBN 0-553-15810-4

Published simultaneously in the United States and Canada

Bantam Books are published by Bantam Books, a division of Bantam Doubleday Dell Publishing Group, Inc. Its trademark, consisting of the words "Bantam Books" and the portrayal of a rooster, is Registered in U.S. Patent and Trademark Office and in other countries. Marca Registrada. Bantam Books, 666 Fifth Avenue, New York, New York 10103.

PRINTED IN THE UNITED STATES OF AMERICA

OPM   0 9 8 7 6 5 4 3 2 1

To Jordana Lane,
with special thanks to Karen Lane

One

◇

"Jessica!" Elizabeth Wakefield exclaimed. "What are you doing?"

"Putting up a poster," Elizabeth's twin sister replied matter-of-factly. Jessica stepped back and smiled at the life-size Johnny Buck poster that she had pinned on the wall across from Elizabeth's bed. Johnny Buck was Jessica's favorite rock star. "Doesn't he look great?"

Elizabeth sighed. Johnny Buck looked fine, but Jessica had pinned the poster over her favorite picture of the famous race horse, Man-of-War. Elizabeth looked at the rest of her sister's mess. Jessica's clothes, cassettes and stuffed animals were scattered all over Elizabeth's usually tidy room. "I guess it's all right," she finally said. "Just don't do anything else without asking me first. OK?"

Jessica flopped down on Elizabeth's bed. "I don't like this any more than you do," she said. She frowned. "*I'm* the one who has to give up my room. And *I'm* the one who has to sleep on the floor!"

Elizabeth sat down beside her twin. "I told you that I'd alternate with you," she reminded Jessica. "We'll each sleep on the floor five nights. That way it'll be fair."

"I don't want to sleep on the floor at all!" Jessica replied. "And I don't want to have to clean my room and drag all my stuff in here." She glanced at the closet, where her short skirts and brightly colored tops were crammed in with Elizabeth's more conservative outfits. "Besides, there's hardly room for even half of my clothes. And I don't know where I'm going to put all my magazines and stuff."

"Well, if you didn't move into my room," Elizabeth pointed out, "Grandma and Grandpa wouldn't have any place to sleep while they're visiting. Anyway, they won't be here that long," she added. "Just ten days."

Elizabeth wished that her grandparents could

stay longer. The last time Grandma and Grandpa Robertson had come they'd taken Elizabeth, Jessica, and Steven, the twins' older brother, to many exciting places, including the circus and the aquarium. But that was a few years ago. Elizabeth was a little worried. Now that Grandma and Grandpa were older, they probably wouldn't be able to do as many things as they'd done before.

After considering what Elizabeth had said, Jessica admitted that ten days was not all that bad. But somehow, she still couldn't be completely positive. "It's not that I don't want to see Grandma and Grandpa," she said defensively. "It's just that the Unicorns have *vitally* important things planned this week, and if I have to spend a lot of time hanging around with Grandpa and Grandma, I'm going to miss something."

Elizabeth looked surprised by her twin's comment. This was one of the times she was reminded of how different they were. Jessica and Elizabeth were identical twins. They both had long blond hair, sparkling blue-green eyes, a dimple in their left cheeks, and tanned, healthy skin from hours in the California sunshine. When they wanted to, they could look so much alike that even their best friends had a hard time telling them apart.

But the twins' personalities were very different. Elizabeth was older than Jessica by four minutes, and the girls often joked that that made her the "older sister." She was the more responsible one and always straightened things out when Jessica got herself into trouble—something that happened fairly often. Elizabeth liked to help out at home and at school, and she liked to spend time with close friends. She was one of the editors of *The Sweet Valley Sixers* and the class treasurer. And with all of that, she still managed to get good grades. Everybody liked Elizabeth.

Jessica was well liked, too, for her bubbly charm and carefree personality. She had many friends, but her best friends were the Unicorns. The Unicorn Club was an exclusive group of the prettiest and most popular girls at the Sweet Valley Middle School. They spent most of their time talking about movie stars, the latest fashions, and the cute boys at school. When Jessica wasn't at a Unicorn meeting, she was usually talking on the telephone with one of the club's members. Every day, Jessica and the other Unicorns tried to wear something purple, the color of royalty, to remind the other kids of just how special they were.

"Do you think," Elizabeth asked, "we'll need to do anything special for Grandma and Grandpa?"

"I hope not," Jessica said. "I'm going to be so busy, I just don't think I'll have the time to—"

"Jessica Wakefield," Elizabeth interrupted, "which is more important to you, Grandma and Grandpa Robertson, or the Unicorns?"

"Well, I certainly hope I'm not going to have to *choose*," Jessica replied. "Grandma and Grandpa will understand that I have other important commitments. I can't hang around and wait on them hand and foot."

Elizabeth shook her head. "Jessica, sometimes I just don't understand you. We haven't seen Grandma and Grandpa for such a long time. I'd think you'd be really excited about their visit."

"I *am* excited," Jessica protested. "But I have a lot of other things to do this week." She began counting them off on her fingers. "On Saturday, Lila Fowler, Ellen Riteman and I are going shopping. On Sunday, Janet Howell is having all the Unicorns over to help plan our next big party. I can't miss that! And on Tuesday, I have to go to—"

"Jessica," Elizabeth interrupted again, "flying all the way from Florida to California is going to be difficult for Grandma and Grandpa. This may be the last visit they're able to make. We have to take advantage of it."

Jessica looked troubled. "OK, but I promised Lila and Ellen that I would—"

Elizabeth held up her hand. "Do you remember that movie we saw on television last weekend?" she asked. "The one about the two old people, living alone and having such a hard time taking care of themselves?"

Jessica nodded. "Sure. But you don't think that *our* grandparents—" She stopped, and her eyes widened. "That's ridiculous, Lizzie! Grandma and Grandpa aren't as old as the people in that film. Those people were *ancient*. They must have been sixty-five, at least."

"Grandma and Grandpa Robertson are in their sixties," Elizabeth said seriously.

Jessica raised her eyebrows. "Wow! I never thought of them as being *that* old."

Elizabeth was thinking about what she had seen in the movie. "Sometimes older people have to eat special food. Sometimes their eyes aren't so good. And sometimes they have trouble walking."

"Remember the time Grandpa was here? Wasn't he limping a little?" Jessica asked thoughtfully.

"That's right," Elizabeth recalled. "His arthritis was bothering him *then*, and that was three or four years ago!"

Jessica flexed her legs, wondering what it felt like to have arthritis. "What do you think we ought to do?" she asked.

"I don't know," Elizabeth said. "I guess we should make things as easy for them as possible."

"If they're *that* old," Jessica said cheerfully, "maybe they won't expect us to go out with them a lot. They'll be just as happy hanging around the house."

"Maybe you're right," Elizabeth agreed. "If Grandpa's arthritis is bothering him, he certainly won't be able to manage those steep stairs at the civic center. I guess we won't be going to the circus this time."

"Hey!" Jessica exclaimed. "Do you think Grandpa will be able to manage *our* stairs? Maybe he and Grandma will decide to sleep downstairs and I'll be able to move back into my room!"

Elizabeth shook her head and got up. "I'm sure Mom wouldn't have suggested an upstairs bedroom if Grandpa couldn't handle stairs." She walked through the bathroom to her twin's room and surveyed the mess. "We'd better get to work, Jess. If we don't hurry, *we'll* be sixty before we get your room ready for Grandma and Grandpa."

Jessica sighed loudly and got up. Why was *she* the one who had to change rooms? She glumly set to work cleaning her room for her grandparents.

Jessica felt more cheerful the next morning. Deep down she was looking forward to her grandparents' visit. She loved to hear stories about her mother as a girl, and she was sure her grandparents would buy her some kind of present. She'd also gotten a wonderful idea while moving all of her things into her sister's room the night before. She had been looking around Elizabeth's dull room and thinking how easy it would be to make it more interesting.

"You're going to do *what*?" Mary Wallace asked Jessica that morning before homeroom. Mary was a seventh-grader, and was friendly with both Jessica and Elizabeth.

"Decorate!" Jessica exclaimed. "Otherwise, I'll be bored out of my mind for ten whole days. I can't stand looking at those plain old walls. Don't tell her, Mary," she added hastily. "It's going to be a surprise."

"But Elizabeth likes her room the way it is," Mary pointed out. "She might not like it if you change things around, especially if it's a surprise."

Jessica smiled confidently. "Elizabeth will like what I'm going to do," she said. "I'm going to think of something fantastic!"

"You always do," Mary said with a grin.

That remark inspired Jessica even more. By the time she walked into homeroom, she was feeling great.

"Hi, Jessica," Lila called out as she came into Mr. Davis's classroom. Lila Fowler was the daughter of one of the wealthier men in Sweet Valley. Next to Elizabeth, she was Jessica's best friend. She was also a member of the Unicorn club. Lila proudly tossed her shoulder-length, light brown hair. Jessica saw a flash of bright silver in her ears. "What's new?" Lila asked Jessica.

Jessica stared at Lila's ears and didn't notice Ellen Riteman walk up to them. "Nothing much," she managed to say.

"What do you think, Jessica?" Ellen asked excitedly. "Aren't they the most outrageous earrings you've ever seen?" Lila was wearing a pair of dangling earrings in the shape of *unicorns*.

Jessica could see that Lila was expecting her to say something. "Yeah, Lila, they're really something," she muttered.

"When are you going to get *your* ears pierced, Jessica?" Lila asked sweetly.

"Jessica can't get hers pierced," Ellen reminded Lila. "Don't you remember? Her mother said she can't. Not for two more years."

Jessica felt herself getting angry. When Lila had gotten her ears pierced, Jessica had asked her parents for permission to do it, too. But they had said she had to wait until she was fourteen! Jessica wanted to get her ears pierced *now*, especially since Lila wasn't about to let her forget she couldn't do something Lila could.

Lila tossed her head again, and her unicorns shone in the light. "Poor Jessica," she said. "It's too bad these earrings don't come in clip-ons. Then you could have a pair, too."

"I'm going to get my ears pierced right away so that I can get some," Ellen said happily. "I'm sure that *all* the Unicorns will want to have earrings just like yours, Lila."

"They're exactly right as a symbol of our club," Lila agreed. "Don't you think so, Jessica?"

Jessica couldn't speak. In a few days, every single one of the Unicorns—except her—would have unicorn earrings. She was relieved when Caroline Pearce came rushing up, interrupting them.

"Have you heard the news?" Caroline announced. "Aaron Dallas is having a party!"

Lila raised her eyebrows. "Are you *sure*, Caroline?" she asked doubtfully.

Jessica knew why Lila was asking. Although Caroline Pearce wrote a gossip column for *The Sweet Valley Sixers*, her information wasn't always accurate.

Caroline looked offended. "Of course I'm sure," she said. "It's going to be a week from Saturday. And it's going to be a very big party. In fact, it's going to be so big that Aaron isn't going to be able to have it at his house!"

"Really?" Ellen asked. "Where is he going to have it?"

"Who is he going to invite?" Jessica wanted to know.

Caroline shrugged. "I don't have any of the details yet, but I'm working on it. When I find out

anything, I'll let you guys know. See you later!"
She dashed off.

"A party!" Jessica exclaimed eagerly. "That
sounds great!"

"This is wonderful!" Ellen said. "I think I'll
get my ears pierced when we go shopping tomorrow. That way, I'll have them done before the
party."

Jessica bit her lip. *Somehow*, she told herself,
*I'm going to have to get Mom and Dad to change their
minds.*

Two

◇

"Just think," Elizabeth said happily at dinner that evening, "in another few hours, Grandma and Grandpa will be here." Her older brother, Steven, nudged her and she passed him the dish of lasagna.

Mrs. Wakefield glanced at Jessica. "Is your room ready for them, Jess?"

Jessica nodded unhappily. "I still don't understand why *I* have to give up *my* room. How come they can't sleep in Steven's room?"

"Then where would I sleep? On the couch?" Steven asked, serving himself a generous second helping of lasagna.

Jessica glared at Steven. Sometimes, he could be an awful pain.

Mr. Wakefield handed Jessica the garlic bread. "Your grandparents are sleeping in your room, Jessica, so let's just end this discussion."

Jessica sighed as she bit into another piece of bread.

Elizabeth looked up from her plate. "Mom, do you think Grandpa is going to be able to manage the stairs?" she asked.

"I certainly hope so," Mrs. Wakefield said, surprised. "What makes you think he couldn't?"

"If he can't," Jessica put in quickly, "maybe he and Grandma could sleep in the den."

Steven laughed. "What's the matter, Jess? Are you afraid that a mouse will come along and nibble your toe if you sleep on the floor?"

Jessica curled her toes up inside her shoes. "Steven Wakefield," she said coldly, "has anyone told you that you are becoming amazingly obnoxious?"

Mrs. Wakefield turned to Elizabeth. "Your grandfather is getting older," she said. "And he has had a touch of arthritis in his knees. But I'm sure that it isn't serious enough to keep him from climbing stairs—at least, not the stairs in our house."

Elizabeth nodded, looking relieved. "That's good," she said.

Jessica looked down at her plate. There was no getting around the fact that she was going to have to sleep on the hard floor in Elizabeth's dull and boring room. Well, that settled it. She was going to have to do some redecorating right away.

Steven shovelled the last of his lasagna into his mouth and gulped down his milk. "Hey, it's getting late," he said, grabbing one more piece of garlic bread. "I've got to get going. The party begins at seven."

"Aren't you going to the airport with us to meet Grandma and Grandpa?" Elizabeth asked.

"Can't," Steven said. He pushed his chair back. "There's a big party tonight at the Hangout."

Jessica suddenly felt envious. "The new teen club?" she asked. She'd heard about the Hangout from Janet, whose brother was in Steven's freshman class at Sweet Valley High. It was supposed to have a terrific dance floor, and it was very popular among the high-school kids. "Hey, that's cool!"

Steven gave her a smart-alecky grin as he got up. "Yeah, and you wish *you* could go, too, don't you? Too bad you're not a couple of years older, Jess. I'll bet you'd really like the Hangout."

"It would be very nice, Steven," Mrs. Wakefield interrupted, "if you could manage to be home by ten tonight."

"Ten?" Steven complained. "But my curfew isn't until eleven!"

"Your grandparents are getting in tonight," Mr. Wakefield pointed out. "I'm sure they would appreciate it if you got home early enough to say hello to them before they go to bed."

"I guess," Steven said in a reluctant voice. "I promise I'll try."

"Try *hard*," Mrs. Wakefield encouraged. She stood up and began to clear the table. "Jessica, isn't it your turn to help me with the dishes tonight? Come on, honey. If we're going to the airport, we'd better hurry."

Jessica sighed. There was nothing she hated more than drying the pots and pans. "Elizabeth," she began, "would you mind . . ."

Elizabeth stood up, too. "Sorry, Jess. I want to finish cleaning our bathroom. Grandma and Grandpa will be using it, and I want to make sure it's spotless."

"Good idea, Elizabeth!" Mrs. Wakefield said. "Come on, Jess."

Jessica got up and followed her mother over to the kitchen sink.

Mom is in a pretty good mood tonight, she thought. *This is a perfect time to ask again about piercing my ears.*

Jessica helped clear the table. She dried the pots and pans and even cleaned off the stove and wiped the counter.

"Well, Jessica, you've done a terrific job," Mrs. Wakefield said when the last pot was put away. "The kitchen is immaculate."

"Thanks, Mom," Jessica said as modestly as she could. "There's something I've been meaning to ask you," she added carelessly, as if the thought had just popped into her head. "Lila just got a pair of new earrings, *unicorn* earrings. All the other Unicorns are going to get them, too. Would it be OK if I got a pair?"

Mrs. Wakefield arched her eyebrows. "Didn't Lila just get her ears pierced?" she asked.

"Yes, she did," Jessica said slowly. She'd been hoping that her mother had forgotten about that.

Mrs. Wakefield smiled. "Well, if you want unicorn earrings, and if you can afford them out of your allowance, I don't see any reason why you can't have them."

Jessica grinned. "Really, Mom? That's won—"

"But of course, Jessica," her mother interrupted, "you'll have to get the clip-on kind, since you don't have pierced ears."

"But Mom," Jessica wailed, "they don't come in clip-ons."

"Then I guess you'll just have to wait to wear them," Mrs. Wakefield said.

Jessica felt like crying. "But all the other Unicorns are getting their ears pierced!" she argued.

Mrs. Wakefield put her arm around Jessica's shoulders and gave her a little hug. "I know you want to get your ears pierced, honey," she said sympathetically. "And I know how hard it is when all the other girls are doing something that you can't do. But I think you're still too young."

"Too young, too young," Jessica grumbled. "It's the story of my life."

Mrs. Wakefield nodded. "I know."

"It's not fair."

Mrs. Wakefield gave Jessica another hug. "Why don't you go see if Elizabeth needs any help getting the bathroom together?" She glanced at the clock. "We have to leave in a few minutes."

Jessica turned away. All the hugs in the world weren't going to make her feel any better. Her mother treated her like a baby!

"Oh, drat," Grandma Robertson said, sitting down on the couch and rubbing her feet. "I'm afraid my ankles are swelling." It was a little after nine that evening, and they had just gotten back from the airport.

Elizabeth and Jessica exchanged worried looks. Then Elizabeth turned to her grandmother. "Would you like to soak your feet?" she asked. "I can get you some warm water and—"

"That's not necessary," Grandma said, wriggling her toes. "I just needed to get out of these shoes. I think they're a size too small." She smiled at Elizabeth. "But you can open that green bag over there and find my slippers, if you don't mind, dear."

Elizabeth hurried over to the suitcase.

Grandpa had sunk into a big chair. "Boy, those airline seats are sure hard on a fellow," he said. "I'm as stiff as a board."

"I know what you mean," Mr. Wakefield agreed. "Those cross-country flights are very long."

Mrs. Wakefield smiled. "It's so good to have you here, Dad." She leaned over and kissed Grandma. "And you, too, Mom. It's been a long time since you've visited us. But you know, you haven't changed a bit. You don't look a *day* older."

Elizabeth thought her grandparents actually looked *many* days older. There were gray streaks in Grandma's hair, and Grandpa had many more wrinkles at the corners of his eyes.

"It *has* been a long time," Grandma said. "Much too long." She smiled happily at the twins. "Just look at my two girls now! They're nearly grown up. They're young ladies!"

Jessica smiled. "Young lady" sounded a bit old-fashioned, but it was nice that Grandma considered them grown up. *With a little help from Grandma Robertson*, Jessica thought, *Mom might even decide I'm old enough to get my ears pierced.*

Mrs. Wakefield turned to Jessica and Elizabeth. "How about getting us all some ice cream, girls? I'm sure Grandpa and Grandma would like some."

"Wait a minute, Alice," Grandpa said. "We don't have to be in such a hurry." He heaved himself to the edge of his chair. "Somewhere in all this luggage, we've got some presents for these two attractive young ladies." He pointed to a suit-case. "Girls, if you'll open that bag, I think you'll find something that might please both of you."

Jessica and Elizabeth grabbed the suitcase at the same time. A minute later, they were unwrapping their presents—a tiny silver heart-shaped locket for Jessica, and Amanda Howard's latest mystery novel for Elizabeth.

"Thank you," Jessica said, hugging her grandmother. "I *love* jewelry, *especially* silver." She cast a look at her mother to see if she had heard, but Mrs. Wakefield didn't seem to have noticed the remark.

"Thank you for the book," Elizabeth told her grandfather. "I can't wait to start reading it."

"I'm glad you like it, honey. Now, how about some of that ice cream?" Grandpa asked, smiling.

"Right away. Come on, Jess," Elizabeth said, heading for the kitchen.

"Well, what do you think?" Elizabeth asked her twin a few minutes later as they were dishing out the ice cream.

Jessica looked down at her locket. "I think it's terrific," she said. Then her smile faded. "I know a pair of earrings that would look perfect with it. If Mom would just let me—"

"I wasn't talking about your locket," Elizabeth said impatiently. "I was talking about Grandma and Grandpa. Do you think they look older?"

"Yes," Jessica said slowly. "Grandma's hair is so gray. And Grandpa is getting kind of chubby around the middle."

Elizabeth put a scoop of ice cream in the last bowl. "They seem tired, too." She shook her head sadly. "I guess we won't be going to a lot of different places this time. I can't really see Grandpa enjoying a day at the aquarium, can you?"

Jessica shook her head. She understood Elizabeth's worry, but there was a bright side. That meant more free time for her to do things with the Unicorns.

When the girls brought the ice cream into the living room, Grandpa looked up with a big grin. "That looks great," he said.

But when Elizabeth put Grandma's dish of ice cream on the coffee table in front of her, she noticed that Grandma's eyes were closed and her head had fallen to one side. She was even snoring a little. Grandma had fallen asleep, and it wasn't even nine-thirty!

Mrs. Wakefield put her finger to her lips so that Elizabeth wouldn't wake Grandma. *Somebody as old as Grandma probably needs lots of rest*, Elizabeth thought. *But still, it's pretty early. Does this mean that Grandma and Grandpa will be going to bed right after dinner every night?* She paused uncertainly. She wondered if she should go get a pillow or a blanket. But before she could decide what to do, Grandma woke up with a start. "My goodness," she said. "I must have dozed off for a few seconds."

"Just for a minute, Mom," Mrs. Wakefield replied gently. "I don't blame you. In Florida, it's past midnight."

Grandpa finished the last spoonful of his ice cream and yawned. "Jet lag," he said, rubbing the back of his neck. "I think I've got a touch of it myself. It won't be long before I'm ready to turn in."

Grandma was looking around. "Has anybody seen my glasses?" she asked.

Elizabeth couldn't help smiling. "They're on top of your head, Grandma," she said.

Grandma felt for her glasses. "I guess they are," she said a little sheepishly. "I have a terrible time remembering where I put them."

"I hope Steven gets back before you and Dad go to bed," Mr. Wakefield said. "He had a party tonight, or he would have come with us to pick you up."

At that moment, a car pulled into the driveway. Mr. Wakefield looked at his watch, and Elizabeth and Jessica traded glances. "I think that's Steven now," their father said, sounding surprised. "He's early!"

Outside, a car door slammed.

Mrs. Wakefield smiled at Grandma. "He must have come home early because he didn't want to miss your first evening with us," she said.

Jessica grinned at Elizabeth. More likely, Steven was home early because he and his latest girlfriend had gotten into an argument.

"I'm looking forward to seeing Steven," Grandma said. "He was terribly handsome when we saw him last, and he had such nice manners, too."

Jessica had to smother a snort. As far as she was concerned, there wasn't *anything* nice about Steven's manners. She thought he was a royal pain in the neck. But that was something that Grandma and Grandpa were sure to find out for themselves during their visit. Steven might be polite at first, but he couldn't hide his true self for very long.

"Steven," Mrs. Wakefield called when they heard him come through the front door, "we're in the living room."

There was a pause. Elizabeth thought that was strange. Steven usually barged into the house. What was he doing?

Mr. Wakefield stood up. "Steven? Hey, Steve! Come on in. Your grandparents are anxious to see you—"

He stopped. Elizabeth and Jessica gasped, and Mrs. Wakefield set down her dish of ice cream with a clatter.

"Steven!" she cried. "Are you *hurt*?"

Steven was standing at the entry to the living room. The sleeve of his shirt was torn. There was a scratch on his face. And his left eye was beginning to turn several shades of purple.

Three

◇

There was a hushed silence. Then both Mrs. Wakefield and Grandma rushed over to Steven. Mrs.
Wakefield touched his eye anxiously. "Are you all
right, Steven?"

Grandma put her hand on Steven's arm where
his sleeve was torn. "Nothing is broken, is it,
dear?"

"No," Steven said. "I'm just a little scratched
up, that's all." He sounded more embarrassed than
hurt.

Jessica glanced at Elizabeth. Steven looked as
if he'd been in a big fight, not as if he was a little
scratched up.

"What in the world happened, Steven?" Mr. Wakefield asked sternly.

Steven let his mother and grandmother lead him to a chair. "Not much, really," he said.

Mrs. Wakefield knelt down to look at Steven's eye. He winced at the touch of her fingers. "I'll get some ice," she said, and headed toward the kitchen.

"It looks to me like you got into a fight, young man," Grandpa said gravely.

"Now, Charles," Grandma said, putting her arm protectively around Steven's shoulders. "Let's not jump to conclusions. Give him a chance to speak for himself."

"Well, Steven? I want to know what happened and I want to know *now*," Mr. Wakefield said.

Steven sighed deeply. "Do you remember the basketball game last Friday? When we beat Big Mesa?"

Mr. Wakefield nodded. Jessica remembered the game. Sweet Valley High had beaten their rival, Big Mesa, by only two points. Steven had scored the winning basket. Even the kids at Sweet Valley Middle School were talking about the game and the fact that a freshman had won it for Sweet Valley High. Jessica hated to admit it, but her brother had been something of a hero all week.

"Well," Steven went on, "we were having a good time at the Hangout, listening to music and dancing and stuff, when a bunch of guys from Big Mesa came barging in. They started making trouble."

"They were still mad about the game?" Jessica asked, leaning forward eagerly.

Steven nodded. "Yeah," he said in a disgusted voice. "They always get mad when we beat them."

"Steven," his father said impatiently, "just tell us what happened."

"Well, they started pushing people around," Steven said. "That wasn't too bad, since the guys they were pushing were big enough to push back. But then they started to pick on Eric Myer. He wasn't a match for those guys, and they knew it. So I . . . well, I got involved."

Elizabeth looked at him. "You mean, you stood up for Eric Myer?"

Steven shrugged. "Yeah," he said nonchalantly. "I mean, I pushed the guy away from Eric. And then somebody hit me, and . . . well, things sort of got out of hand after that."

"I didn't know the Hangout was that kind of place," Mr. Wakefield said. "It's obvious that they don't have the right kind of supervision over there.''

"Yes, I'm surprised," Mrs. Wakefield said, as she came back into the living room with a small bag of ice. "Everybody's been talking about what a great place it is for the kids. But from what Steven's told us tonight, I'd say it isn't as great as we thought it was.''

"It wasn't the Hangout's fault, Mom," Steven said, putting the ice bag on his eye. "It was those guys from Big Mesa. They're the ones who started it."

"Well, all's well that end's well," Grandma said cheerfully. She straightened up. "Alice, where would you like us to sleep? It's time for us to be getting to bed.''

Elizabeth spoke up. "You're sleeping upstairs, in Jessica's room," she said. She glanced at Grandpa. "That's OK, isn't it?''

"Sounds fine to me," Grandpa said. He started to get one of the suitcases, but Elizabeth beat him to it.

"Let me carry it, Grandpa," she said. "It looks really heavy.''

Grandpa laughed. "If you're sure you can manage it, honey.''

Not to be outdone by her twin, Jessica took Grandma's suitcase, and the four of them went up the stairs. At the door of her room, Jessica noticed that a few of her tapes were still in the middle of the floor. While Elizabeth was showing Grandma and Grandpa her room, Jessica pushed the tapes under the bed and arranged the bed ruffle so that nobody could see the mess underneath.

Later, when Elizabeth was getting into bed and Jessica was crawling into her sleeping bag, she said wearily, "Poor Grandpa. Did you see how long it took him to get up the stairs, Lizzie? He was moving one step at a time."

"Uh-huh," Elizabeth agreed sleepily. "And did you notice how forgetful Grandma was with her glasses?"

"I guess that's what happens when people get old," Jessica said through a yawn. "They forget things."

"I guess," Elizabeth replied.

On Saturday morning, Elizabeth got up extra early, before anyone else was awake. Leaving Jessica curled up in bed, she went downstairs to the kitchen. The Wakefields got up late on Saturday mornings. Usually they ate cold cereal or fixed whatever they wanted, but Elizabeth had decided she would make breakfast this morning. First she went into the backyard and picked some white daisies for the table. Then she set the table and put the daisies in a vase in the center of it. As an afterthought, she draped a shawl over one chair. If Grandma got cold she could cover her shoulders with it. Finally, Elizabeth began to cook.

Elizabeth was putting the finishing touches on breakfast when Steven came into the room. His eye wasn't different shades of purple this morning; now it was black and very puffy.

"Hey," he asked, "what's with all this fancy stuff?"

Elizabeth got the orange juice out of the refrigerator. "I thought we ought to do something nice for Grandma and Grandpa," she said. "After all, it's their first breakfast with us."

Steven glanced hungrily toward the stove. Steven's enormous appetite was a Wakefield family joke. "So what are you making?" he asked eagerly.

"Oatmeal," she said. "And soft-boiled eggs."

"What?" Steven groaned. "Oatmeal? I can't eat that stuff! And soft-boiled eggs are for babies!"

Elizabeth gave him a disgusted look. "Well, you don't have to eat it, you know. You can always find something for yourself."

"Thanks," Steven said, snatching an apple from a bowl on the counter. "Maybe I will." He slapped together a few peanut butter sandwiches, grabbed a banana, and tucked a small bottle of fruit juice under his arm. "Bye," he said. "I'm going to basketball practice." A second later, he was out the door.

Jessica came downstairs next. She was already dressed in jeans and a pink sweatshirt, and her hair was tied with a pink ribbon.

"Oh, good," she said, looking at the table approvingly. "Breakfast. Did you cook?"

Elizabeth nodded happily. "I thought I'd surprise everybody." She set a glass of juice beside each plate.

"What are we having? French toast with maple syrup? Pancakes?" Jessica took the lid off the pan on the stove. "What is this?"

"Oatmeal."

"Oatmeal!" Jessica slammed down the lid. "*Yuck!* What else are we having?"

"Soft-boiled eggs."

"Soft-boiled eggs!" Jessica cried. "And oatmeal! Elizabeth, what are you trying to do? Poison us?"

Elizabeth turned around. "Jessica Wakefield," she said sternly, "will you stop thinking about yourself for a change? You may not appreciate this breakfast, but Grandma and Grandpa will. Oatmeal or soft-boiled eggs don't upset the digestive system."

Jessica grimaced. "Oatmeal upsets *my* digestive system," she said. "I hope I never get old." She picked up her glass of orange juice and gulped it down. "I'm going to Lila's," she said. "If I hurry, maybe I can eat with her. I bet *she's* having something edible for breakfast."

Elizabeth sighed. Oatmeal and soft-boiled eggs weren't exactly her favorites either. But when her grandparents came down for breakfast, they seemed to like what she had done.

"Ah," Grandpa said, "oatmeal." He sat down and shook out his napkin. "Sort of reminds me of when I was growing up, back on the farm. My mother cooked oatmeal every morning." He chuckled. "And if we didn't eat it, we got a good—"

"You've set a lovely table, Elizabeth," Grandma said hurriedly. "The daisies are very cheerful."

Elizabeth spent the rest of the morning retrieving eyeglasses, slippers, and magazines for her grandparents. She did everything she could to make them comfortable, including covering grandpa with a blanket when he fell asleep.

Just before noon, Grandpa woke up and pushed himself out of his chair. He stood up and stretched. "Well," he said, "I guess it's time for my exercise." He peered at Elizabeth over his glasses. "How about you, Lizzie? Do any running?"

Elizabeth stared at him. "Running?" she managed to say.

Grandpa jogged a few quick steps in place. "You know, jogging."

"Sometimes I do," Elizabeth said uncertainly. "Sometimes Dad and I jog together."

Grandma put down her knitting. "Maybe a quick run would be good for me, too, Charles," she said. "I'll find our jogging suits." She turned to Elizabeth. "For our last wedding anniversary, we bought matching jogging suits. Bright red ones!"

Grandpa grinned at her. "Are you coming, Elizabeth? A few quick turns around the block will be good for all of us."

Elizabeth couldn't believe what she was hearing. Her grandfather and grandmother jogging around the block? "But what about your arthritis?"

she demanded. "Last night you seemed awfully stiff."

"Last night we spent six hours on an airplane," Grandma reminded her. "Even your young knees would be stiff if you'd had to sit that long, honey."

"Doc says a little exercise is good for the old bones," Grandpa said cheerfully. He pounded his chest. "The ticker, too. And it sure wouldn't hurt if I'd lose a pound or two. Come on, Liz, get your running shoes. I'll bet I can beat you around the block."

And ten minutes later, he very nearly did.

Jessica, Lila, and Ellen had just finished eating breakfast at Lila's. Lila's housekeeper, Mrs. Pervis, had fixed a wonderful meal and Jessica had stuffed herself. She explained that breakfast at her house was disgusting.

"Poor Jessica," Lila said. "It's really too bad that you have to put up with your grandfather and grandmother for ten whole days. My grandmother visited once. It was totally boring."

Jessica shrugged. "It's really not so bad," she said. "They're pretty nice." She fingered the locket they had given her. "But they're getting old and a little creaky. And the worst part of the whole thing is having to sleep in Elizabeth's room."

"Hurry up, you guys," Ellen interrupted. "I want to go to the mall."

Lila laughed. "You're just anxious to get your ears pierced so that you can have a pair of unicorn earrings."

"That's right!" Ellen confirmed. She looked at Jessica. "Did you ask your mother again? What did she say?"

Jessica sighed. "What do you think she said? She said no."

Ellen made a face. "Poor Jessica."

Jessica stood up. "Listen, I'm tired of hearing you guys say poor Jessica," she said. "If we're going shopping, let's go!"

The mall was crowded. Ellen and Lila wanted to go to the jewelry store right away, so Ellen could get her ears pierced immediately. Jessica didn't want to go with them. She thought it would be humiliating to have to stand by and watch Ellen get her ears pierced when *she* wouldn't be able to do it for two entire years. It might as well be forever.

"I'm going to Barton's," Jessica announced as soon as they got to the fountain in the middle of the mall. "I need to buy a few things to fix up Elizabeth's room this weekend."

Lila laughed. "I'm sure Elizabeth's room needs it. I bet she'll *love* your decorating," she said sarcastically.

"She won't mind," Jessica said confidently. "Besides, I'm the one who had to move out of my room. And I'm only going to make one or two minor changes."

Lila consulted her watch. "Well, then, how about if we meet back here at the fountain in half an hour?"

Jessica nodded. When the others had gone, she turned and went into Barton's. There, she bought a half-dozen of the latest movie star and rock magazines, several packages of purple thumbtacks, and a big spool of beautiful purple ribbon. She was going to make a wall collage on one wall of Elizabeth's room. First she would cut interesting pictures and funny captions out of the magazines. Then she would tack the pictures and captions to the wall at interesting angles. The purple ribbon, tacked diagonally across the wall, would make the perfect finishing touch. Jessica couldn't wait to get started on the project. She knew it would look incredible when she finished. She was sure Elizabeth would agree.

Buying the things at Barton's only took about fifteen minutes. Jessica window-shopped for a little while. She bought a chocolate shake to take her mind off Ellen's silver unicorn earrings.

A few minutes before she was supposed to meet Lila and Ellen, she went to the fountain to wait. She was sitting there, leafing through one of her new magazines, when a shadow fell across the page.

"Hi, Jessica," a boy's voice said.

Jessica looked up. It was Todd Wilkins. Jessica had always thought he was adorable. The only problem was that Todd didn't seem to be interested in girls. But at that very moment, he was standing in front of her with his hands in his pockets, smiling shyly.

"Hi, Todd," Jessica said.

"Are you and your sister shopping?" Todd asked

"Elizabeth isn't, but I am," Jessica said. "I'm supposed to meet Lila and Ellen in a few minutes."

"Oh," Todd said. "Well, in that case, I guess I'll let you go."

"You're not—" Jessica began, but Todd was already turning away.

"See you later," he said over his shoulder. A minute later, he had vanished into the crowd.

"Wasn't that Todd Wilkins?" Lila asked eagerly, coming up to Jessica.

"See my ears?" Ellen asked, leaning forward so that Jessica could see that she was wearing tiny gold earrings. "They wouldn't let me put the unicorns in right away. But I have them right here." She held up a little bag. "Want to see them?"

Jessica ignored Ellen. "Yes, that was Todd," she told Lila.

"What did he *want*?" Lila asked.

"What do you think of my ears, Jessica?" Ellen persisted.

Lila turned on her. "Ellen, will you be quiet about your ears for a minute? I want to hear what Todd said to Jessica. Come on, Jessica," Lila went on. "Tell us about it."

Jessica put on a mysterious smile. "He just stopped to talk for a few minutes, that's all," she said calmly. "You know, about things. About Aaron Dallas's party. No big deal."

"No big deal?" Lila squealed. "Jessica, I think Todd Wilkins is so *cute*. And he *never* talks to girls.

What did he say about the party? Did he tell you anything about where it was going to be, or anything like that?"

"No, he just wanted to talk, that's all," Jessica repeated. She was pleased that Todd had come up at just that moment. Now Lila was so excited about him that she'd forgotten all about Ellen's newly pierced ears.

Jessica was excited about Todd, too—but she wasn't going to let Lila and Ellen know that.

Four

◇

"Did you say *jogging*?" Jessica asked incredulously.

Elizabeth was tying her running shoes. "I didn't believe it either," she said. "But I guess Grandma and Grandpa aren't quite as old as we thought." She grinned. "In fact, I heard Grandpa talking to Dad at breakfast about getting up a game of golf, and Grandma told Mom she wanted to do a few laps in the pool. Can you *believe* it?"

Jessica giggled. "Does that mean you won't be cooking any more oatmeal and soft-boiled eggs?"

"I guess not," Elizabeth replied, blushing a little. "I feel kind of silly. I really went overboard, didn't I?" She straightened up. "Want to run with us, Jess? Mom and Dad are coming, too. We're going to stop at the park and feed the ducks."

Jessica shook her head. She would have gone with them, but she had something else she wanted to do that morning. If she hurried, she might get it finished before her twin and everyone else got back.

"No, thanks," she said. And then she added, "How well do you know Todd Wilkins?"

Elizabeth hesitated. "Todd? Well enough, I guess. Why?"

"Do you think he's cute?"

"Cute?" Elizabeth looked thoughtful. "Well, I hadn't really thought about it, but sure. I think he's cute." She glanced at Jessica curiously. "What makes you ask?"

Jessica gave a little sigh of disappointment. It was never any fun talking to Elizabeth about boys. She just wasn't interested. "No reason," Jessica replied in an offhand tone.

Elizabeth shrugged. "Sure you won't come jogging with us?"

"I'm sure," Jessica said, glancing toward the closet, where she'd stuffed the magazines and the ribbon. "I've got something to do."

Two hours later, Jessica was just finishing her project, when she heard Elizabeth and the others coming in downstairs. Hurriedly, she shoved most of the scraps of paper and ribbon under Elizabeth's bed. Then she stood up to admire what she had done. Her fingers were stiff from cutting out so many pictures and sore from poking in hundreds of thumbtacks.

But it had all been worth it. The collage looked terrific. Best of all, there was a picture of the Unicorns standing with rock star Donny Diamond right at the center of it. The picture had been taken just a few weeks before, when Donny Diamond had played at their school dance. Yards of purple ribbon crisscrossed all the pictures. Jessica smiled with satisfaction. The collage was just the thing Elizabeth's room had needed.

"Jessica," Mrs. Wakefield called, "are you going to hide out upstairs all day? Why don't you come down and sit with us?"

"OK," Jessica said reluctantly. She stuffed the rest of the magazines in the top drawer of Elizabeth's dresser, and went downstairs. She decided that it would probably be a good idea to leave the house before Elizabeth saw her room. Although

Jessica was sure Elizabeth would like it, her twin might need some time to get used to it.

But it was very hard to escape. As it turned out, Grandpa had recently read an article about rock music and he wanted to hear about Jessica's favorite groups. It was difficult to explain Donny Diamond's music to somebody who admitted that he'd never even heard of him. And she couldn't say much about Johnny Buck when her grandfather already confessed that he didn't care for loud music.

"Well, what about this folksinger, Darcy somebody-or-other?" Grandpa asked. "I heard one of her songs on the radio the other day, and I liked it."

Jessica was surprised. "Darcy Campman? You liked Darcy Campman? She's giving a benefit concert here soon."

"Yes, I liked her. I could understand the words, and I didn't even have to turn her down." Grandpa laughed.

Jessica sighed. Talking to her grandfather about music was hopeless.

Grandma laughed a little. "Back in our day, it was Frank Sinatra that everybody was crazy about.

And Glenn Miller, of course. We loved dancing to Glen Miller."

Grandpa grinned at her. "Bing Crosby, too. Do you remember the time we went to the Bing Crosby concert in Chicago? If I recall, we spent most of the week's grocery money on those tickets." He paused, shaking his head. "Johnny Buck, Donny Diamond—those new guys ought to listen to Bing Crosby. He knew how to sing a song, and he didn't blast out your eardrums, either."

Jessica sighed. She'd seen Frank Sinatra and Bing Crosby in old movies on television. Nobody listened to their music anymore. She smiled at the idea that Johnny Buck and Donny Diamond could learn anything from anyone so old.

Just then, Elizabeth came downstairs. "Grandma and Grandpa," she said grimly, "would you mind if I interrupted you? There's something I have to ask Jessica."

Jessica looked up. There was a tone in Elizabeth's voice that she wasn't sure she liked. The next minute, her twin had pulled her into the hallway.

"Jessica Wakefield," Elizabeth demanded, "who gave you permission to tack all that *junk* on my wall?"

"Junk?" Jessica exclaimed. "That's not junk, Lizzie. Those are pictures of the most famous—"

"It looks *awful*! And all that purple ribbon, too!"

"I think it looks nice. I thought you would, too," Jessica replied. "Anyway, if you don't like it, you can take it all down when I move out."

"But when I take it down there will be little *holes* all over my wall," Elizabeth complained.

Jessica frowned. "Well, I had to do *something*," she said. "I don't know how you can live with those boring walls, Lizzie. I really did think you'd like it." She looked at her twin hopefully. "You're not mad, are you?"

Elizabeth exhaled loudly. "No. I just wish you'd asked 'me first. You left scraps of paper *everywhere*."

"I'll clean it up," Jessica promised. She stole another glance at her twin. "Uh, by the way, Lizzie, isn't it your turn to sleep on the floor tonight?"

Elizabeth sighed again.

On Monday, all of the sixth-graders were talking about Aaron Dallas's party, which was the following Saturday. In fact, there was so much gossip about the party that almost nobody paid any attention to Ellen's pierced ears. She went around all morning with a hurt look on her face.

It was during gym class that Jessica and the Unicorns finally found out exactly where Aaron was going to have his party.

"It's going to be at the Hangout," Caroline Pearce announced excitedly.

"The *Hangout*!" Lila exclaimed. "Then it must be a big party."

"The biggest," Caroline said happily. "Aaron is inviting the whole sixth grade and a lot of the seventh-graders, too."

"All right!" Ellen said. "That means Bruce Patman is coming!" The Unicorns thought Bruce was the cutest boy in seventh grade.

"But wait. There's more!" Caroline said. She leaned forward, dropping her voice. "Dave Carlquist is going to be there, playing records."

"*The* Dave Carlquist?" Jessica cried in delight. "I can't believe it!"

All the Unicorns agreed that Aaron's party was going to be the best event of the year. It was the very first big boy-girl party outside of school or somebody's house.

At lunch, Jessica was standing at the end of the line, waiting for Lila and Ellen, when Todd passed by.

"Hi, Jessica," he said. "Have you heard about Aaron's party?"

Jessica nodded. "Doesn't it sound like fun?"

"Yes, it does," Todd said. His brown eyes held her gaze and Jessica's heart skipped a beat. "So are you and your sister going to be there?"

"*I* wouldn't miss it for the world," she said, flashing him a flirtatious look. "Are you going?"

"Sure," Todd said casually. "I wouldn't miss it either. I'm glad you'll both be there." He gave her a shy smile, and walked away.

A moment later, Lila and Ellen hurried up. "What did he want *this* time?" Lila asked eagerly.

"Nothing special," Jessica said, trying to contain her excitement. "He just wanted to talk about the party."

Ellen's eyes widened. "The party? He didn't ask you for a *date*, did he?"

"No, not exactly," Jessica admitted. "But he did want to make sure I'd be there. He said that he wouldn't miss the party, especially since I would be there."

"Well, that's practically asking for a date," Lila said authoritatively.

"I wouldn't exactly say that," Jessica said modestly. But for the rest of the day, whenever she thought about Aaron's party and Todd Wilkins, she could feel her face get warm.

"Dave Carlquist is bound to remember you, Elizabeth," Amy said that afternoon as they were getting ready to go home. "After all, *you* were the one who came up with the winning name for his radio show."

Elizabeth nodded happily. Dave had picked her suggestion, "The Awesome Hour," as the winner in a contest he had sponsored a few months ago. She'd even gotten to be on the radio with him. It had been very exciting. She'd liked Dave, and she was looking forward to seeing him again.

On the way home, Jessica and Elizabeth talked about Aaron's party. Jessica told Elizabeth what Todd had said.

Elizabeth gave her twin a questioning look. "Did Todd ask you to go to the party with him?" she asked.

Jessica shook her head. "No," she admitted. "But it does sort of sound like he might be *thinking* of asking me, doesn't it?"

"Well, maybe," Elizabeth said.

Jessica grinned. "I can't *wait* to tell Steven that the party's going to be at the Hangout. He's bragged so much about that place." Then she frowned. "Maybe we'd better not make a big deal about it in front of Mom and Dad," she said. "Not after what happened to Steven there on Friday night."

"But that wasn't Steven's fault," Elizabeth pointed out. "Those guys at Big Mesa started the fight because they're such poor losers. It doesn't have anything to do with us or the Hangout."

Jessica nodded. "You and I know that," she said. "But I'm not so sure about Mom and Dad."

When the twins got home, they hurried into the kitchen to tell their mother about the party. They conveniently forgot to mention that it was going to be held at the Hangout.

"It sounds like it's going to be a great party, girls," Mrs. Wakefield said. Grandma, who was peeling potatoes for dinner, agreed that it sounded like fun, especially when Elizabeth told her about Dave Carlquist.

"We didn't have parties like that when I was growing up," she said. Elizabeth thought she sounded wistful.

Jessica grinned at her grandmother. "Was that before they invented record players?" she asked mischievously.

Grandma laughed and tossed a potato peel at her as she and Elizabeth ran out of the room. Jessica went straight upstairs to call Lila and Ellen and talk about the party.

At supper that night, Grandma told Grandpa about Aaron Dallas's party. "And there's even going to be a disk jockey," she added.

"It sounds like a pretty big deal," Grandpa said with interest.

"It *is!*" Jessica exclaimed. "*Everybody's* going to be there." She thought about Todd.

"A disk jockey?" Steven asked incredulously. "There's going to be a disk jockey?"

"Dave Carlquist," Elizabeth told him.

Steven whistled. "Hey, not bad," he said approvingly. "That should be *some* party. Where's it going to be? In the gym at school?"

Elizabeth and Jessica traded looks.

"That's right, girls," Mrs. Wakefield said. "You've told us everything about the party except where it's going to be held. The Dallases have a large house, but I don't think it's *that* big."

"Well, actually . . ." Jessica hesitated, and then began shredding her napkin. She exchanged a troubled glance with her twin.

Mr. Wakefield leaned forward. "Jessica, just exactly where is this party going to be held?"

Elizabeth looked down at her plate, suddenly feeling apprehensive. "It's at the Hangout," she said quietly.

"The Hangout?" Mr. and Mrs. Wakefield exclaimed at the same time.

No one said anything for a long time. At last Mrs. Wakefield spoke. "I'm very sorry, girls, but your father and I can't let you go to a party at that place. Not after what happened to Steven."

Elizabeth stared at her mother in dismay. "But, Mom . . ."

"Your mother's right," Mr. Wakefield agreed. "There's no supervision at that club." He looked at both of them. "I think you guessed what our reaction would be," he added. "That must be why you didn't want to tell us where it's being held."

"But we *have* to go, Dad!" Jessica cried. "We *can't* miss this party! It's the most important party ever!"

"Jessica's right," Elizabeth said. "It *is* an important party. All the sixth-graders are going to be there."

Mrs. Wakefield shook her head regretfully. "That may be true, Elizabeth. But we can't have you girls going somewhere that isn't safe."

"And that's all there is to it," Mr. Wakefield added in his firmest voice. "You're not going."

Five

◇

"I can't believe it," Jessica cried. She paced up and down the kitchen while Elizabeth washed the dishes. "This is the worst thing that's ever happened to me in my whole life. I just can't believe that they won't let me go to the party, Lizzie! I'll be the only sixth-grader who's not there!"

Elizabeth put a casserole dish in the sink to soak. "No, you won't," she said. "I won't be there either."

Jessica sank down in a chair. "Well, it's not fair," she said angrily. "Mom and Dad don't trust us. They're treating us like babies because they don't think we've got the sense to take care of ourselves."

Elizabeth sighed. "I don't think it's a matter of trusting *us*," she said. "It's the other kids at the Hangout that they don't trust."

Jessica's eyes flashed. "It's so unfair! They're ruining our lives because of something we didn't do!" She stopped pacing and glared at Elizabeth. "They're not my bosses. I'm twelve years old, and they can't tell me what to do! *We're* twelve years old," she corrected herself. "They can't tell *us* what to do."

"What's our alternative?" Elizabeth asked quietly.

"I don't know," Jessica replied. "This is terrible. *We* weren't the ones who got into that fight. This whole thing is Steven's fault."

"No, it isn't," Elizabeth defended him. "Steven didn't start the fight. He was trying to help someone. Besides, who could have guessed that those guys from Big Mesa would cause trouble?"

Steven came into the kitchen. "So," he said, "you guys don't get to go to the party after all, huh?"

Jessica jumped up. "Maybe you can fix things," she said hopefully. "Maybe you could talk to Mom and get her to change her mind."

"Mom and Dad seem to have their minds

made up on this one," Steven said seriously. "I'm beginning to think they won't ever let *me* go to the Hangout either."

"It's this way all the time." Jessica flung out her arms with a dramatic gesture. "They're just doing this to keep me from doing something I want to do! Something that's *crucial*! Something that everybody else gets to do! If they had their way, I'd live in a jailhouse!"

Steven grinned at Jessica's melodrama. "*Everything* you want to do is crucial, Jess. Every time you don't get what you want, you think the world is coming to an end."

"They don't say no very often," Elizabeth reminded her twin.

"They say no all the time," Jessica insisted. "In fact, just today Mom said I couldn't get my ears pierced."

Steven snorted. "Why anyone in her right mind would want to get holes punched in her ears is beyond me. I think it's idiotic!"

"Lila got her ears pierced," Jessica replied. "So did Ellen. Pretty soon, all the other Unicorns will have their ears pierced—all of them except me."

Steven shrugged. "That doesn't make it any less dumb."

"You're just saying that because you're a boy," Jessica said hotly. "Boys never understand *anything*. They're completely and totally dense."

"Are you calling me stupid?" Steven growled.

Elizabeth stepped in. "Stop it, you guys," she said. "Steven, Jessica's right about one thing. We're being punished for something that neither one of us is responsible for. And I really don't think the Hangout is a dangerous place, do you?"

Steven shook his head. "There's plenty of supervision. The minute the fight started last Friday, they hustled all the troublemakers out." He grinned ruefully. "Including me."

"Have you told Mom and Dad that?" Elizabeth asked.

"Sure. Lots of times." Steven stuffed his hands in his pockets. "But it didn't do any good. I'm telling you, Liz, their minds are made up on this one."

"Well, we've got to do *something*," Jessica moaned. "I'll never be able to face Lila and Ellen again if I don't get to go to the party! They'll really think I'm a baby then. I'm too young to get my ears pierced, and I'm too young to go to the biggest, best party ever!" Jessica's voice rose to a wail. "I'm ruined!"

Under other circumstances, Elizabeth might have been tempted to giggle. But the truth was, she understood exactly how Jessica felt.

All the rest of that night and again Tuesday morning, Jessica thought about the party on Saturday night. There had to be a way to convince her parents to let them go. But even though Jessica was usually able to come up with a foolproof scheme, this time she couldn't think of anything.

She was in the bathroom brushing her teeth before school and trying to think of how she was going to tell the Unicorns she couldn't go to the party. She decided that the best strategy was not to let her friends know how awful she was feeling.

At that moment, her grandmother came in. "Mind if I use the mirror, honey?" she said. "I'm getting dressed to go out for the day with your grandfather, and I need the mirror to put my earrings in."

Jessica turned around in surprise. "I hadn't noticed that you have pierced ears, Grandma."

She watched her grandmother slip a pair of small, gold hoop earrings into her ears.

Grandma smiled at Jessica's reflection in the mirror. There was a twinkle in Grandma's blue-green eyes. "I got them pierced when I was . . . oh, about your age, Jessica."

"You did?" Jessica was astonished. "You mean, your mother let you get it done when you were only twelve?"

"Actually, I was the first of all my friends to do it," Grandma said. "I always liked being a little ahead of the crowd. And in my town, at that time, getting your ears pierced was rather a daring thing to do."

Jessica gave her grandmother a thoughtful look. "I'll bet all your friends were jealous," she remarked. "Did they rush right out and do it, too?"

Grandma laughed. "How did you guess? My mother said it was like measles, a real epidemic. Everybody wanted to be a copycat. But of course, there's nothing wrong with that," she added. "All of the other girls wanted pretty earrings, just like mine."

Jessica put her toothbrush away. "So what do you think about twelve-year-olds getting their ears pierced *these* days?" she asked in a tone that was overly casual.

"I don't see any difference between then and now," Grandma replied. "At least, not when it comes to pierced ears."

"So you think it would be all right if . . . if somebody did that," Jessica persisted. "When she was twelve years old, I mean."

"I don't see why not," Grandma said.

"You can't go to Aaron's party?" Ellen cried.

Jessica nodded as calmly as she could, trying not to show how upset she was.

"Jessica, I can't believe your parents would be so old-fashioned," Lila said disapprovingly. "Your grandparents probably had something to do with this."

"No, not really," Jessica replied with a shrug. "It was all because of the fight at the Hangout last Friday night. Steven got a black eye. So Mom and Dad have decided that the Hangout isn't safe."

Ellen nodded knowingly. "I heard all about that fight. The whole school's been talking about it." She paused. "Are you going to tell Todd Wilkins that you can't go?"

Jessica bit her lip. She hadn't thought of that.

"Well, I think your parents are treating you like a baby," Lila said.

She tossed her head, and her silver unicorn earrings danced. "Why do you stand for this kind of thing, Jessica?" Lila asked. "Last week it was getting your ears pierced. This week it's going to the party. What will it be next?"

Jessica didn't answer.

"You *are* twelve years old," Lila went on, "practically a teenager. You don't have to take this. Why don't you just tell them off?"

Jessica sighed. She wasn't surprised that Lila didn't understand. Lila's father was rarely home, and when he was, Lila could twist him around her little finger. She had no idea of what it was like to live with *real* parents, the kind who didn't spoil you rotten.

"Lila's right," Ellen added. "Your parents should be treating you like a grown-up, not a child. You should do something, Jessica. You shouldn't just sit around and take it."

Jessica was silent. It was easy for *them* to say.

"You can't go?" Amy Sutton asked in disbelief. "But why not?"

"Because of what happened to Steven," Elizabeth replied.

"But that didn't have anything to do with *you*," Amy pointed out. "It's so unfair!"

"I know," Elizabeth said. "But there's no use complaining about how unfair it is. That's not going to change my parents' minds."

"I guess not," Amy agreed. "So what are you going to do?"

"I don't know," Elizabeth admitted. "I suppose I'll try to talk to them again. Maybe after Mom's had some time to think about it . . ." Her voice trailed off. Elizabeth wasn't hopeful that her parents would change their decision.

Amy put her arm around Elizabeth's shoulders. "Well, the party probably won't be such a big deal, anyway," she said comfortingly. "You know how it is. When you look forward to something the way everybody's looking forward to this party, it always turns out to be a disappointment. No party can be as terrific as everybody is making this out to be."

Elizabeth nodded. She knew Amy was just trying to make her feel better. She managed a smile for Amy's benefit. "You're probably right," she said. "I probably won't be missing very much."

Amy quickly changed the subject. But five minutes later, she was talking to Mary Wallace about what she was going to wear to the party.

"Mom says I can buy a new outfit," Mary said happily. "What about you?"

"Maybe I'll ask my mom if I can have something new, too," Amy replied. She turned to Elizabeth. "What are you—" She clapped her hand over her mouth, a stricken look on her face.

"What's wrong?" Mary asked.

"I can't go to the party," Elizabeth replied miserably. "My parents won't let me."

"Elizabeth!" Mary exclaimed. "That's terrible!"

Elizabeth couldn't have agreed more.

Jessica was standing by the drinking fountain when Todd came over. "Is it true?" he asked. "Your parents won't let you and Elizabeth go to Aaron's party?"

"Todd," Jessica said slowly, stalling for time. "Where did you hear that?" She didn't want Todd to think her parents were treating her like an infant.

"Caroline Pearce told me," Todd said. "You mean, it isn't true?"

Jessica smiled. "Poor Caroline. She gets things so mixed up, especially when it comes to my sister and me. Sometimes she can't tell us apart."

"So it's Elizabeth who can't go?"

Jessica flipped her hair back. "You see, Elizabeth was supposed to do something, and she didn't, and . . . well, my parents . . ." She let her voice trail off.

Todd nodded. "I guess I'll see you Saturday night, then." He jammed his hands into his pockets and walked away quietly.

"Did you tell him you can't go?" Lila asked after she joined Jessica in the hall. "What did he say?"

Jessica shook her head. "He thinks it's Elizabeth who can't go." She narrowed her eyes. "And don't you tell him anything different, Lila Fowler."

"Why did you lie?" Lila asked. "When you're not at the party, he'll know that Caroline was telling the truth."

"I'll figure something out," Jessica said. "There's got to be a way."

Six

"Mom," Elizabeth said Tuesday evening as she was chopping celery for the salad, "could we talk about the party?"

Mrs. Wakefield turned from the stove. "You mean, the one Aaron is having at the Hangout?" She emphasized the last two words.

Elizabeth's heart sank. It sounded as if her mother's mind was still made up.

"I've been talking to some of the kids," Elizabeth began. "They all say that what happened last Friday night was a fluke. Nothing like that has ever happened at the Hangout before, and it's not very likely that it will ever happen again."

Mrs. Wakefield sighed. "I know that you think

I'm being unfair, Elizabeth. But when you have a daughter of your own, you'll see the situation from a different point of view. Your father and I are worried about your safety, that's all."

Elizabeth pushed the celery into a bowl. "But I'm trying to tell you that the Hangout *is* a safe place," she argued. "There really isn't anything to worry about. Lots of parents let their kids go there."

"That may be," Mrs. Wakefield replied. "But you're *our* daughter, and we're not 'lots of parents.' "

"Mom," Elizabeth said quietly, "I think you and Dad are being too protective. After all, Jessica and I are twelve years old. We're not babies."

Her mother gave her a very small smile. "You know, Elizabeth, I remember saying something like that to *my* mother when I was about your age," she said. "But I see things differently now that I have you girls. Parents have to be protective, and sometimes their children don't understand why." She shook her head. "I'm sorry for the way things have turned out, honey. I'm sorry you have to miss the party. But the answer is still no."

Elizabeth would have liked to be able to tell her mother that she understood, but the truth was, she didn't. She still thought her mother was overreacting to what had happened.

*   *   *

Wednesday was a terrible day for Jessica. It seemed as if Lila and Ellen were making a special effort to talk about the party in front of her.

"Are you going to wear your purple sweater to the party on Saturday night?" Lila asked Ellen in a loud voice, so Jessica couldn't possibly miss hearing.

Jessica spent the entire day feeling like she would burst into tears if somebody said just one more word about Aaron's party. Something very special was going to happen on Saturday night and she wasn't going to be there to enjoy it.

Jessica felt so miserable about the party that nothing was fun. She couldn't understand how Elizabeth could enjoy sitting around talking to Grandma and Grandpa. Jessica was bored with watching her grandmother knit, and she was tired of Grandpa's stories about the good old days.

"If I have to listen to one more story about how much fun it was to milk the cows, I'll scream," she said, when Elizabeth came up to their room that evening and tried to persuade her to come back downstairs.

"But nobody's talking about cows," Elizabeth said. "Grandma just told a funny story about the time she sneaked out of her dorm after curfew so she and Grandpa could go for a moonlight walk. Mom and Dad thought it was hilarious. Even Steven laughed!"

Jessica made a face. "What's so funny about sneaking out to go for a walk?"

"Grandma and Grandpa are *asking* about you, Jess," Elizabeth said quietly. "They've been wondering why you're not spending more time with them."

Jessica shrugged. "Tell them I'm doing homework or something," she said. "Really, Elizabeth, Grandma, Grandpa, and I don't have a single thing in common."

Elizabeth just turned around and left the room. Downstairs, she reported that Jessica was buried under a pile of homework.

"My goodness," Grandma said, "that girl really does study hard." She looked at Elizabeth. "We're not keeping you from your homework, are we, Elizabeth?"

Elizabeth shook her head. "I got mine done after school," she said. A minute later, they heard Jessica giggling on the phone. Grandpa raised his eyebrows. Grandma shook her head at him, and Elizabeth was glad they didn't say anything. For once, she didn't feel like defending her twin.

*   *   *

"Don't forget," Elizabeth reminded Jessica as they were getting ready for school on Thursday, "today's the day we're going to the aquarium with Grandma and Grandpa."

Jessica groaned. "Ugh. You can go if you want," she said. "I'm not."

"You're not going?" Elizabeth asked, surprised. "Why? We had so much fun the last time. Remember how much we liked watching the dolphins?"

Jessica put down her hairbrush. "If any of the Unicorns ever saw my grandparents escorting me around the aquarium like a baby, I'd never be able to show my face in school again."

Elizabeth stared at her. "A baby!" she exclaimed. "That's crazy, Jessica. They're our *grandparents*! Everybody goes out with their grandparents once in a while. And anyway," she added, "they're taking us out for pizza afterward. You don't want to miss *that*, do you?"

"I can have pizza anytime," Jessica said.

"What are you going to tell them?" Elizabeth wanted to know. "They're expecting you to go with us. They've been looking forward to it all week."

"I'm not going to tell them anything," Jessica

replied decisively. "*You* are going to tell them that I'm at Janet's, at a vitally important meeting. And you can tell them that I'm terribly, terribly sorry, too," she added.

Elizabeth was tired of making excuses for Jessica, but she decided that it wouldn't do any good to argue with her twin. She couldn't change the way Jessica behaved.

When she got home from school that afternoon, Elizabeth repeated to her grandparents what Jessica had told her that morning.

"What a shame." Grandma sighed sadly. "I was looking forward to having her along. We just haven't seen enough of her."

Grandpa shook his head. "That girl has more things to do than anyone else I know," he said with a frown.

Just as they were about to leave for the aquarium, the phone rang. Grandma reached for it. When she hung up, there was a hurt expression on her face.

"Who was it?" Grandpa asked.

"It was Janet Howell," Grandma said quietly, "with an important message for Jessica. She said to tell Jessica that she wants Jessica to be in charge of the decorations for the next party. She'll expect a report at the Unicorn meeting next week."

Elizabeth couldn't say a word.

After a moment, Grandpa said, "I see." Then he put his arm around Elizabeth's shoulders. "Listen, it's time to have some fun," he said. "Come on, Liz. I want to see what those otters are up to, and I don't want to wait a second longer."

But when they got to the aquarium, they were unpleasantly surprised.

"Closed for repairs!" Grandma exclaimed, looking at the sign on the aquarium gate and shaking her head. "What luck."

Elizabeth peered through the bars into the patio entryway. Except for some sea gulls sunning themselves on a railing, the place was deserted.

"Closed!" she said sorrowfully. Somehow it seemed like the last straw. All week she had looked forward to this trip, as a substitute for the party.

Grandpa tried to be cheerful. "Don't I remember that there's a local history museum somewhere nearby, Elizabeth?" he asked.

Grandma put her hand on Elizabeth's shoulder. "There's no use crying over spilled milk," she said. "Let's go to the museum."

So they went. But it wasn't the same, and even though Elizabeth tried to enjoy herself, she couldn't help feeling miserable.

*   *   *

On Friday, Jessica, Lila, and Ellen went to the mall right after school. Lila wanted to buy a new pair of shoes for the party, and Ellen was looking for a new belt. Jessica didn't want to go along, but she thought that if she went home, she would have to spend a dull afternoon with Elizabeth and their grandparents.

"I've got it all figured out," Lila said, as the girls entered the mall.

"What have you got figured out?" Jessica wanted to know.

"Why your parents are being so strict with you," Lila replied.

"I think it's because they want to keep her a baby forever," Ellen put in.

"Well, maybe," Lila agreed. "But if you ask me, it's because your grandparents are visiting. I think your mother wants to show *her* mother what a great mother she is."

Jessica stared at Lila. That was something she hadn't thought of. But now that Lila mentioned it, it made perfect sense. *Why did they choose this time to visit?* she thought angrily.

"Well, whatever the reason, the fact is, your parents just don't seem to understand that twelve is practically grown up," Ellen remarked.

"You're absolutely right," Jessica said firmly, her mind suddenly made up. "And I'm not going to take it a minute longer."

Lila raised her eyebrows. "You're not? What are you going to do?"

"Well, for starters," Jessica said, "I'm going to get my ears pierced."

"You *are*?" Ellen asked. "But aren't you afraid of what your parents will do? I mean, they'll be really mad."

"Who cares?" Jessica stated defiantly. "They've already made me miserable by telling me that I can't go to Aaron's party. Whatever they do to me for getting my ears pierced can't be any worse than that."

"That's the spirit, Jessica!" Lila exclaimed.

Ellen looked impressed. "You've got a lot of nerve," she remarked.

"Well," Jessica said calmly, "why are we standing around? Come on, let's go! I want my pair of silver unicorn earrings!"

Seven

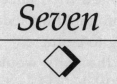

"Mom," Elizabeth said, "I need to talk to you about the party."

It was Friday night, and Elizabeth had decided that she had to try to talk to her mother one more time. Her mother was in the den, looking through a color chart. Mrs. Wakefield worked part-time for an interior design studio in Sweet Valley, and she often brought her work home with her.

Mrs. Wakefield put the color chart down. "Oh, Elizabeth." She sighed heavily. "Do we have to talk about this again?"

Elizabeth took a deep breath. "But, Mom, I want to tell you something that you probably don't know. If you did, it might make you change your mind about not letting us go."

"All right, Elizabeth," Mrs. Wakefield said. "What is it about this party that I don't know?"

"Well," Elizabeth said, "the party is going to be very well chaperoned." She cast a hopeful look at her mother to see what effect this information would have. "Aaron told me today that both of his parents are going to be there."

"I assumed the party would be chaperoned, Elizabeth," Mrs. Wakefield said patiently.

"But what could happen with *two* chaperones right there?" Elizabeth argued desperately. "All the other parents must think it's safe, or they wouldn't be letting their kids go!"

"I told you, Elizabeth. We're not 'all the other parents.' We're *your* parents," Mrs. Wakefield replied, sounding a little exasperated. "And anyway, you never can tell what might happen. What if some high-school boys came in and—"

"No high-school boy is going to crash a middle-school party!" Elizabeth protested. "They wouldn't be caught dead there."

"Even when Dave Carlquist is there?" her mother asked quietly. "He's very popular, and I'm sure a lot of high-school students are fans of his."

Elizabeth frowned. "I'm sure Dave Carlquist would never let any trouble start."

"Probably not. But he won't be watching every minute. After what happened to Steven at the Hangout, I just can't risk it," Mrs. Wakefield said firmly.

It was hopeless to try to change her mind. Elizabeth bit her lip and tried not to cry. At that moment, Grandma came into the den.

"I came to see if you wanted me to do anything for dinner," she said. Seeing Elizabeth's stricken face, she looked concerned. "What's the matter, Elizabeth? Did something happen at school today?"

Elizabeth lowered her head. She was afraid that if she tried to talk, she would burst into tears.

"She's upset about not being able to go to the party," Mrs. Wakefield said shortly. She put her color chart into a file folder.

Grandma put her arm around Elizabeth's shoulder. "That's OK, honey," she murmured. "This isn't the only party in the world. There'll be others."

"Not like this one," Elizabeth said in a low tone. Her voice was trembling. "This one is special. Dave Carlquist is going to be there."

There was silence for a minute, and then

Grandma spoke up. "I don't mean to interfere, Alice, but don't you think that perhaps—"

Mrs. Wakefield picked up her briefcase and put it on the desk. "Mother," she said evenly, "please don't get involved in this."

Elizabeth held her breath, not daring to move. Was Grandma going to try to change her mother's mind?

Grandma spoke again. "Really, Alice, I think that you and Ned are being just a bit too strict."

"Please, Mother," Mrs. Wakefield said. "Ned and I are doing what we think is best for the girls. I'm not a child any longer and I certainly don't need to be told how to raise my own children." She snapped open her briefcase and put the file folder inside.

Elizabeth was surprised. When her mother had said *I'm not a child any longer*, she had sounded exactly like Jessica.

"I know you're not a child," Grandma replied. There was a slight edge in her voice.

Elizabeth blinked. Grandma had sounded exactly like her mother when she was talking to Jessica.

"Well, then, don't treat me like one," Mrs. Wakefield replied.

"I don't intend to," Grandma answered. "And I certainly don't want to upset you. But the girls are such *good* girls, and it just seems to me that . . ."

Mrs. Wakefield sighed. "Yes, the twins *are* good. But this doesn't have anything to do with their behavior. It has to do with the place where the party is being held." She shook her head. "I don't want to talk about it anymore, Mom. The girls are *not* going to that party, and that's all there is to it."

"I suppose you know best." Grandma sighed. She gave Elizabeth a comforting squeeze. "Well, Elizabeth," she added, "we'll just have to think of something else to do tomorrow evening. Tell you what. Why don't you and Jessica put your heads together, and come up with something exciting. Maybe there's a movie you've been wanting to see, or a new restaurant you'd like to try."

Elizabeth's shoulders sagged. If Grandma couldn't get her mother to change her mind, that was the end of it. There was absolutely no hope. And whatever they did instead, however exciting it was, it couldn't make up for missing the party.

"Where is everybody?" Mr. Wakefield called from the front hall. "I'm home."

"Oh, good," Alice Wakefield said. She glanced

at her watch. "Ned and I were thinking that perhaps we could all go out to dinner tonight. What do you say, Mom?"

"That would be nice," Grandma agreed.

Elizabeth's father came into the den. "Is anybody in the mood for Mexican food?" He looked around. "I saw Steven outside, but where's Jessica?"

The door opened. "I'm here," Jessica said. Her cheeks were flushed a little and her hair was fluffed forward around her face.

"Wonderful," Mrs. Wakefield said cheerfully. "We're all home. Well, what do you think? Would Mexican food—" She stopped, and then went across the room to look closely at Jessica. "What's wrong, Jessica?"

Jessica tossed her head. Elizabeth gasped. Her twin was wearing little gold earrings in her ears!

"I got my ears pierced," Jessica said defiantly. Her voice shook a little, but she folded her arms in an I-don't-care-what-you-think gesture.

"After I told you you couldn't?" Mrs. Wakefield asked, her voice rising. "You deliberately disobeyed me!" Elizabeth couldn't remember ever seeing her mother so angry.

Mr. Wakefield frowned. "And just what do you think we ought to do to punish you, Jessica?"

Jessica shrugged. "I don't know," she said. "You've already told me I can't go to Aaron's party tomorrow night. What worse punishment is there?"

Even though Jessica looked and sounded confident, Elizabeth suspected that her twin was already beginning to regret what she had done. If there had been the slightest chance of their being allowed to go to the party, it was gone now. Jessica had completely ruined their chances.

"Well, I'm sure *I* can think of some sort of appropriate punishment," Mrs. Wakefield snapped. "To start, let's say you're grounded for a month."

Mr. Wakefield raised his eyebrows. "A month? I think we ought to make it two."

Elizabeth gasped. None of them had ever been grounded for that long before!

Jessica's eyes widened in dismay. "Two months!" she wailed. "But two months is *forever!*"

Mrs. Wakefield shook her head. "I'm sorry, Jessica," she said. "But two months it is."

Grandma cleared her throat uneasily. "I'm afraid," she said, "that this is my doing."

"Your doing?" Mrs. Wakefield exclaimed. "I don't understand."

Grandma sighed. "I didn't mean to, Alice, and I certainly wish I hadn't." She glanced at Jessica. "But you see, Jessica and I were talking about how old I was when I got *my* ears pierced. I'm afraid I gave her the idea that it was all right for a twelve-year-old to do it."

Elizabeth glanced at Jessica. Her twin was smiling slightly.

Mr. Wakefield sighed. "Jessica has been wanting to do this since before you arrived. You certainly didn't give her the idea."

"That may be," Grandma said, sounding a bit disgruntled. "But the fact remains that I practically gave her my permission to do it. I didn't know that the two of you had strong feelings against it."

"Jessica knew," Mrs. Wakefield said emphatically. "She could have told you."

"Perhaps," Grandma agreed. "But that doesn't change the fact that I told her I thought it would be all right. I do feel that I'm more to blame than Jessica is, Alice. I wish you and Ned wouldn't punish her so severely."

There was a long silence. Finally, Mrs. Wakefield spoke up. "Well, you may have a point. If Jessica got the idea from you that getting her ears pierced was acceptable, I don't see how we can punish her for it."

Mr. Wakefield laughed. "And we certainly can't punish *you*."

Grandma laughed, too. She crossed the room and gave Mrs. Wakefield a hug. "Maybe you ought to punish me, Alice," she said. "For interfering too much."

"That's right," Mrs. Wakefield agreed. "We should punish you." And then she said, "OK, Mom, you're grounded."

Elizabeth grinned at the look of surprise on her grandmother's face.

"All right!" Jessica said. "Way to go, Mom!"

"I've wanted to say that ever since *I* was twelve!" Mrs. Wakefield exclaimed. They all laughed.

"Does this mean I'm not grounded?" Jessica asked quickly.

"I guess," Mrs. Wakefield said. She frowned. "But I still think what you did was wrong, Jessica. And what's more, I think you know it."

"Your mom's right," Mr. Wakefield said. "But if your grandmother said it was all right, I don't see how we can punish you."

Jessica heaved a sigh of relief. "Thanks, Mom and Dad," she said jubilantly. "Thanks, Grandma."

Grandma frowned. "I don't want any thanks, Jessica. I did something I shouldn't have."

But Jessica wasn't listening. She was running up the stairs two at a time. She couldn't wait to phone Lila and tell her what had happened.

Later that night, the girls were upstairs, getting ready for bed. Elizabeth was putting on her pajamas and Jessica was brushing her hair in front of the mirror.

Jessica tossed her hair back to show off her earrings. "Well, Lizzie," she said in a pleased voice, "what do you think?"

"They're OK, I guess," Elizabeth said.

Jessica gave her a pitying look. "Getting your ears pierced is a sign of maturity," she informed her sister.

"Maybe." Elizabeth laughed. "Does this mean I have to give up my status as older sister? You got your ears pierced, so I guess that makes you more grown up."

"You could get your ears pierced, too," Jessica said. "Mom couldn't say no to you, after she let *me* get away with it." Her face became thoughtful. "If you had pierced ears, we'd have twice as many pairs of earrings, and we could trade all the time."

"Sorry, Jessica," Elizabeth said. "I don't want to get my ears pierced. For one thing, it probably hurts."

Jessica put down the brush and turned around. "No, honestly Lizzie, it didn't hurt a *bit*. They use this little machine. It's over in a second. It's a lot less painful than when we got our shots for school."

Elizabeth looked skeptical. "I don't think I'm ready to try it. Anyway, I've got bigger problems to deal with."

Jessica suddenly looked glum. "Such as the party."

"Such as the party," Elizabeth agreed dismally. "I tried again tonight to talk to Mom. Grandma even stood up for us. But the answer is still no." She frowned. "I would never have believed Mom could be so unreasonable. But she won't budge a single inch."

"Grandma stood up for us?" Jessica asked.

Elizabeth nodded. "She told Mom that she and Dad were being too strict."

Jessica's eyes widened. "Grandma actually said that?"

"Yes. But it didn't do any good. Mom asked her not to interfere, and Grandma agreed not to. We can forget about any help from her."

There was a knock on the door and then Grandma slowly opened it. "I just want to say good night, girls," she said.

Jessica got up and ran across the room to give her grandmother a hug. "Thanks again for what you did tonight," she said gratefully. "It's wonderful not to be grounded." She stepped back and gave her grandmother a curious look. "But why did you cover for me? It would have been just as easy to let Mom punish me."

Grandma frowned. "I certainly wasn't 'covering' for you, Jessica. But I believe that when you make a mistake, you have to be mature enough to take responsibility for what you've done. I stepped in because I feel that I was somewhat responsible for what happened. I had to take a stand. But I do think you should apologize to your mother."

"I will apologize," Jessica promised earnestly. "I'll do it tomorrow."

Elizabeth looked at her grandmother. "I guess I just never noticed that you have pierced ears," she said. "Is it true that you had it done when you were twelve?"

Grandma nodded. "It's true," she said. She made a face. "It hurt like the dickens, too. Served me right, I guess."

"It hurt?" Jessica asked, surprised. "But it didn't hurt me."

"I'm sure they have more modern ways to do it now," Grandma told her. "But back when I was a girl, it wasn't easy or painless."

"How did you do it?" Elizabeth asked. "Did your doctor do it for you?"

Grandma laughed. "To tell the truth," she said, "a friend of mine did it, in her mother's kitchen. With a sterilized needle, an ice cube, a cork, and some thread."

Jessica's face went pale. "A *needle*?" she gasped, putting her hand over her mouth. "Oh, how horrible. I think I'm going to be sick."

"But the pain wasn't the worst part," Grandma went on. She sighed. "You see, I got in a lot of trouble when I got home." She shook her head, remembering.

Jessica looked at her in surprise. "You mean, your mother punished *you*?"

"Did she *ever*," Grandma said fervently. "She was very strict, and she had told me that I had to wait until I was sixteen before I got my ears pierced.

I wish I'd told you that part, Jessica," she added. "Hearing about my punishment might have changed your mind."

"What was your punishment?" Elizabeth wanted to know.

"Double chores." Grandma sighed. "Not only did I have to wash and dry the dishes, but I had to make the beds every day and scrub the floors once a week for a whole month. On top of that, I was grounded for a month. I missed the county fair that summer. Everyone got to go except me."

Jessica couldn't help laughing. It was funny to hear her grandmother talk about getting in trouble. Somehow, she hadn't imagined that her grandmother had ever been her age.

Elizabeth looked thoughtfully at her grandmother. "Were you and Grandpa strict with Mom when she was growing up?" she asked.

Grandma thought for a minute. "Yes, I think we were," she said. "From what I've seen while we've been here, I believe that Grandpa and I were stricter than your parents are." She paused. "I know that when your mother was a girl, she thought we were *much* too strict. She complained about not getting to do things that her friends got to do."

Jessica stared at her. "She did?" After a minute she added, "Did she ever get in trouble?"

Grandma put her arm around Jessica's shoulders and hugged her. "Sometimes," she said with a little laugh. "Sometimes *she* got grounded, too, just the way I did when I was a girl. And sometimes we had to tell her that we didn't want her to go someplace that she had her heart set on." Her face clouded over a little. "I'm sure your mother was terribly disappointed, just the way the two of you have been this week."

Elizabeth sighed. For a little while, she had been able to forget about the party. She wished that Grandma hadn't reminded her.

Eight

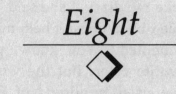

"Any luck?" Amy asked Elizabeth on Saturday morning. She had come over to talk to her friend and see if the news about the chaperones would change the Wakefields' decision.

"No," Elizabeth sighed, leading Amy up the stairs to her room. "Mom said she'd already assumed that the party would be chaperoned. It didn't make any difference."

"Elizabeth, can't she see how *unfair* she's being?" Amy asked. "She's just not listening to reason on this thing. She . . ."

Amy trailed off as she stood in the doorway of Elizabeth's room. "*What,*" she said distastefully, "is *that*?" She pointed to the wall Jessica had decorated.

Elizabeth laughed. "That," she replied, "is Jessica's idea of a good way to liven up a boring room."

Amy blinked. "All those pictures tilted every which way make me dizzy," she said.

"The purple ribbon doesn't help much either," Elizabeth commented. "You know, purple isn't exactly my favorite color. But the worst of it is, Jess must have used hundreds of thumbtacks. When she takes it down, there'll be little holes all over the wall."

"When *is* she taking it down?" Amy asked. "Soon, I hope."

"In two days," Elizabeth replied. "As soon as Grandma and Grandpa are gone and she can move back into her room." She looked around at the messy room. Jessica's clothes were everywhere. Her skates were lying on the middle of the bed, and magazines and cassette tapes covered the floor. "I have to admit that I'll be glad," she added, "even though I wish Grandma and Grandpa didn't have to go to San Diego so soon."

"Are they going to see your cousin Robin?" Amy asked.

"Yes," Elizabeth said. "I wish Jess and I could go, too. It's been a long time since we've seen

Robin. We had so much fun the last time we were all together. But I'm sure Mom and Dad wouldn't let us go unless they came along."

"Probably not," Amy agreed. "If they think you're too young to go to a party at the Hangout, they'd definitely think you're too young to go all the way to San Diego." She paused. "The party tonight won't be half as much fun without you there."

Out in the yard, Jessica was helping Mrs. Wakefield clean out one of the flower beds. On Saturdays, Jessica usually went over to Lila's or Ellen's, but this morning she had something to tell her mother.

Jessica leaned on her rake. "Mom," she began, "I think I owe you an apology. For what happened yesterday, I mean."

Mrs. Wakefield sat back on her heels. "Yes," she said calmly, "I think you do."

Jessica bit her lip. "I wish I hadn't done it," she said softly.

"I wish you hadn't, too," her mother replied. "To tell you the truth, though, it's not the pierced ears that bothers me so much. What *really* bothers me is that I'm afraid I will find it hard to trust you after you deliberately disobeyed me."

Jessica stared at her mother. "Oh, but you *can* trust me!" she cried.

"Are you sure?" her mother asked quietly.

Jessica looked down. "Well, if Grandma hadn't said it was OK to get your ears pierced when you're twelve, I never would have done it. Anyway," she added, "I apologize."

"I accept," Mrs. Wakefield said. "By the way, I meant to tell you that your father and I have to go out tonight. Some of his clients are in town for the evening, and we're going to take them out to dinner. We may be out late."

"Mm-mm-m," Jessica said. She stopped raking. "Listen, Mom," she added earnestly, "speaking of tonight, I want to talk to you about Aaron's party."

Mrs. Wakefield looked up. A hint of laughter glinted in her eyes. "Jessica, if you're about to ask me to let you go to the party at the Hangout tonight, I'd have to say that you have a remarkably poor sense of timing. Don't you agree?"

"But, Mom—" Jessica began plaintively.

"Sorry, honey," her mother replied. "The answer is still no."

Suddenly, Jessica lost her temper. "You don't *care* that I'm humiliated, and that everybody's laughing at me behind my back!" she cried, flinging the rake down on the ground. "You don't *care* that all the Unicorns think I'm a baby because my parents won't let me go to the absolutely, positively *best* party in the whole wide world!"

Her mother didn't answer. She turned back to the flower bed.

Being ignored just made Jessica more angry. "You're not being *fair!*" she accused. "You are being totally *unfair.*"

There was a dry cough behind her, and then a voice said, "Excuse me, Jessica."

Jessica whirled around. Her grandfather was standing on the patio. He wore a pained look on his face.

At any other time, Jessica might have been ashamed that her grandfather had seen her making such a scene. But right now, she was too angry and upset to be ashamed.

"There's a telephone call for you, dear," her grandfather told her. "It's Lila." He turned and went back into the house.

Jessica was still angry when she picked up the phone. "Hello, Lila," she snapped. "What do you want?"

"Jessica," Lila gushed happily, ignoring Jessica's tone. "You can't *guess* what I just bought!"

"What now?" Jessica asked. Lila bought so many things—from clothes to stereos to a television set for her room—that it was impossible to guess what it might be this time.

"Oh, come on, guess," Lila urged.

"I can't," Jessica replied glumly. "I don't feel like guessing. Just tell me what it is."

"A new outfit, for the party tonight!" Lila exclaimed. "I can't *wait* to show it to you!" she went on. "It's the palest shade of purple, with a black velvet collar and sash. And best of all, it has a little unicorn embroidered on the front! I can't believe how perfect it is!"

"Shut up, Lila!" Jessica said crossly.

There was a moment's silence. When Lila spoke again, her voice was frosty. "Jessica Wakefield, you're just mad because your parents won't let you go to the party. You don't need to go out of your way to make me feel bad, just because you do."

"If anybody's trying to make anybody feel bad," Jessica shot back, "it's you, Lila. All week long, you've talked about nothing but the party. You know I can't go, and you've rubbed it in every chance you got. That's why you called to tell me about your dress. You wanted to rub it in again." She was a little surprised by what she heard herself saying.

"Well, Jessica," Lila answered haughtily, "you're certainly entitled to your opinion. But my opinion is that if you're not going to the party, it's entirely your own fault. If I were you, and somebody told me I couldn't go, I'd do something about it."

Jessica was tired of hearing Lila talk. "Lila," she said coldly, "I would appreciate it if you would tell me exactly *what* you would do."

"Well, it's obvious," Lila said. "I'd sneak out."

Jessica was silent.

"And if I had a sister," Lila went on, "I'd make her agree to sneak out with me, so that she couldn't tell. But of course," Lila added condescendingly, "you'd probably be afraid to do something like that."

"No, I wouldn't," Jessica retorted. "I wasn't afraid to get my ears pierced after my mom and dad said I couldn't, was I?"

"Well?" Lila asked archly.

Jessica didn't reply right away. After a moment she said, "Listen, Lila, I'll talk to you later, OK?"

"But I wanted to tell you about the rest of my

new outfit," Lila protested. "I got the greatest sandals and—"

"I've got to go now," Jessica said. "Goodbye, Lila." She put down the receiver, but she didn't get up right away. She just sat there, staring off into space.

Amy had gone and Elizabeth was sitting on her bed, looking around at her messy room. Aaron's party was going to be starting in a few hours. The closer it got, the worse Elizabeth felt. The door opened and Jessica came in. She was wearing what Elizabeth recognized as her scheming look.

"Lizzie," Jessica announced, "we've got to do something about the party tonight."

"I told you, Jess," Elizabeth replied. "I've already talked to Mom. Twice. It's hopeless."

"I know," Jessica said. "I tried this morning, too."

Elizabeth nodded. "I heard you. I think everyone heard you."

Jessica gave her a sour look. "I lost my temper," she said.

Elizabeth shrugged. "I guess it doesn't matter," she said. "Even if you hadn't lost your temper, you probably couldn't have changed Mom's mind."

Jessica flopped down at the foot of the bed. "Well, I've come to a decision," she said. "I'm going to that party, no matter what Mom and Dad say."

Elizabeth frowned at her sister. "And just how are you going to manage that?"

"I'm going to sneak out," Jessica said calmly.

Elizabeth's eyes widened. "Sneak out?"

"And I want you to come with me."

"Are you crazy?" Elizabeth asked.

"No, I'm not crazy." Jessica sat up and folded her arms across her chest. "I'm tired of being treated like a baby. Come on, admit it, Elizabeth. Mom and Dad are being completely unreasonable about this, aren't they?"

"Yes," Elizabeth said slowly. "They're not being fair."

Jessica nodded. "We deserve to go to that party, don't we?" She fingered her gold earrings a little sheepishly. "Well, *you* do, anyway."

"I guess," Elizabeth said after a minute.

Jessica looked satisfied. "So we should just go, no matter what they say."

Elizabeth shook her head. "We can't just *go*," she said.

"Why not?" Jessica demanded.

"Because," Elizabeth said, without much conviction, "it's not right. And anyway, we'd get caught," she added.

"No, we won't!" Jessica said firmly. "I've got it all figured out. Mom told me that she and Dad have to go to dinner with some of Dad's clients. Grandma and Grandpa will go to bed pretty early. All we have to do is wait until they're asleep and just walk out the front door." She laughed. "We won't have to sneak out, really. All we have to do is come back before Dad and Mom get home."

Elizabeth stared at Jessica. She made it sound so easy. And Elizabeth didn't want to stay home, when everybody else would be seeing Dave Carlquist.

"Come on, Lizzie," Jessica urged. "Let's do it! Everybody at school will admire us for having the courage to stand up to our parents!"

"But we wouldn't exactly be standing up to them," Elizabeth pointed out. "We'd be sneaking around behind their backs. There's nothing very courageous about that."

"Whatever," Jessica said impatiently. "At least we wouldn't be taking their orders."

"And there's something else, too," Elizabeth said. "It wouldn't be right to treat Grandma and Grandpa that way, either. They trust us."

"Don't be silly!" Jessica cried. "I'll bet Grandma would do exactly what we're doing if she were us. Didn't she tell you a story about sneaking out of her college dorm after hours? If *she* can do it, we can, too!"

Elizabeth felt herself wavering.

"Come on, Lizzie," Jessica pleaded. "Please say yes. And stop worrying about Grandma and Grandpa. They'll be asleep. They won't know anything about it!"

Just then, Elizabeth heard a cough. When she looked up, she saw Grandpa standing in the door of the bathroom that joined her room to Jessica's. Grandma was right behind him.

Jessica gasped out loud. Elizabeth was stunned. She stared at her grandparents. "Did you . . ." She stopped and tried again. "Have you been standing there long?"

"Long enough," Grandpa said shortly.

"We heard everything," Grandma said. "And I don't mind telling you that we're *very* upset."

Nine

"Oh, no," Jessica moaned.

"I'm sorry," Elizabeth said quickly.

"We didn't intend to listen in on your conversation," Grandpa said. "But now that we've heard it, the question is, what are we going to do?"

Jessica pulled the pillow off her head. "Do?" she asked faintly. "Couldn't we . . . well, couldn't we just sort of forget about it?"

"I think this is too serious to forget about," Grandma said in a grave voice. She looked at Grandpa. "Don't you agree, Charles?"

Grandpa looked first at Jessica, then at Elizabeth. He shook his head sorrowfully. "Sneaking out is very serious," he said.

"But you sneaked out, Grandma!" Jessica cried, sitting up straight. "You sneaked out of your dorm after hours to go for a walk with Grandpa! And you thought it was just a joke!"

"Just because I did something a very long time ago doesn't make it right for you to do now, Jessica," Grandma said reprovingly. She shook her head at Grandpa. "You know, Charles, I'm not so sure it's a good idea to tell the girls stories about the scrapes we used to get ourselves into. It seems to give them ideas."

"I don't believe," Grandpa said with a sober look, "that Jessica got the idea for sneaking out from you, Marjorie. I think it's something she came up with all by herself."

Jessica lowered her head. "Actually, it was Lila's idea," she muttered. "She suggested it."

"Lila!" Elizabeth turned to stare at her twin. "You mean, you and Lila came up with this plan? And then you tried to drag me into it?" She paused, the truth beginning to dawn on her. "What did you need me for, Jess? To make sure that I wouldn't tell on you?"

Jessica's eyes filled with tears. "No, Elizabeth! I mean, Lila did suggest that you and I should both sneak out. But . . ." Jessica stopped, biting her lip. She was silent for a minute. Then a change seemed to come over her. She cast a quick glance at her grandparents and squared her shoulders bravely.

"The whole thing was my idea," she confessed in a dramatic voice. "It's not right for me to blame Lila or use Grandma's story about sneaking out as an excuse. I want to take full responsibility." Her shoulders seemed to sag just the tiniest bit. "And I have to face up to the consequences, whatever they may be. I just hope that you take the circumstances into consideration."

Elizabeth almost smiled. What an actress her twin was! She couldn't help hoping that her twin would convince their grandparents. If she didn't, they would both be in deep trouble.

Grandma was nodding approvingly, obviously impressed with Jessica's change of heart. "I'm glad to hear you say that you take responsibility, Jessica. That's a very adult way of handling this."

"Yes, Grandma," Jessica said meekly, looking down at her hands.

"I'm glad to hear that you intend to face up to the consequences." Grandpa's voice was gruff and his face was creased with a frown. "Elizabeth, is that how you feel, too?"

Elizabeth sighed. "Yes, Grandpa." Even though Jessica had done a masterful job of acting, it didn't look like her effort had done any good at all. His frown showed that Grandpa wasn't letting up one bit.

"Well, good," Grandpa replied. "Now, I think we'd better go downstairs and talk to your parents about what's just happened."

"Tell Dad and Mom?" Jessica cried in a horrified voice, her acting forgotten. "Please, no!"

Elizabeth gulped. There was a sick feeling in her stomach.

"It's really the best thing, Jessica," Grandma said. "We need to have this out in the open."

"But, Grandma!" Jessica wailed desperately. "They'll *kill* us!"

"Oh, come now, Jessica," Grandpa said with a slight twinkle in his eyes. "I don't think they'll go that far."

"They'll ground us forever!" Jessica moaned.

"If you tell them that you take full responsibility and that you're ready to face the consequences of your actions," Grandma pointed out reasonably, "you might be surprised at their response."

Jessica's eyes were full of tears.

Grandpa put his hand on her shoulder. "Come on, girls, let's go," he said. "The sooner we get it over with, the better for everybody."

Slowly and reluctantly, Elizabeth followed the three of them downstairs. Her stomach hurt and she wondered if she was going to be sick. Jessica was always getting into trouble with their parents, so she was used to things like this. But Elizabeth hardly ever did. Planning to sneak out was probably the worst thing she had ever done.

Mrs. Wakefield was reading the paper in the living room when they all came into the room. She put down the paper when she saw them.

"Where's Ned?" Grandpa asked.

"Right here," Mr. Wakefield said, coming into the room. "What's up?"

"Something happened just now," Grandma said, with a glance at the twins, "that we think you ought to know about."

Elizabeth and Jessica looked at each other unhappily. This was going to be bad.

"What is it?" Mr. Wakefield asked. He looked at the girls. "Is there something wrong?"

"Yes, what is it?" Mrs. Wakefield said. "You all look so serious."

"It is serious, Alice," Grandpa said. "You see, a few minutes ago, your mother and I overheard Jessica and Elizabeth plotting."

Mr. and Mrs. Wakefield looked puzzled.

"They were planning to sneak out and go to the party tonight," Grandpa continued. "While you two were at dinner and we were in bed."

"Sneak out!" Mrs. Wakefield exclaimed, horrified.

Mr. Wakefield looked from Jessica to Elizabeth. "That *is* serious," he said with a frown.

"You see," Grandpa went on, putting his hand on Elizabeth's shoulder, "the girls couldn't figure out why you were being so unfair about the party. They felt they were being punished by not being permitted to go. And they didn't feel they had done anything to be punished for." He glanced at Jessica. "At least, not so severely."

"Knowing that all their friends were going made it much worse," Grandma put in. "All the other parents obviously thought the Hangout was a safe place to have a party, so they thought you were being unreasonable."

"But you saw Steven's eye!" Mrs. Wakefield exclaimed. "He might have been hurt very badly in that fight!"

"And we heard Steven's explanation," Grandpa replied thoughtfully. "It didn't sound to us like something that was likely to happen again."

"I'm not sure what you're trying to get at," Mr. Wakefield said.

Grandma stepped forward. "The two of us have been here since this thing started, Ned. We've seen enough to be able to put all the pieces together. When we overheard the girls talking about their feelings, we felt you really ought to know what we think."

"Yes," Grandpa said, "we have to tell you it's our feeling that Jessica and Elizabeth should be allowed to go to the party."

Jessica gasped in surprise. Elizabeth was totally speechless. This was something she had never expected.

"Well, I must say, Mom," Mrs. Wakefield exclaimed, "that I'm a bit surprised. As a matter of fact, you're the very last person I would have expected to hear this from."

"I know," Grandma said. Elizabeth thought she heard a touch of sadness in her voice. "We all learn as we grow older, dear."

Mr. Wakefield looked at Mrs. Wakefield. "Well," he said, "perhaps there *is* a different way to look at this situation." He glanced sternly back at Jessica. "Still, sneaking out is no way to solve the problem. I'm really disappointed that the girls would even consider such a thing."

Jessica's sigh was audible in the long pause.

A signal passed between the twins' parents. Then Mrs. Wakefield spoke. "If you don't mind, everyone, Ned and I would like to talk this over—in the kitchen."

"Not a bad idea," Grandpa said affably. "I think I'm in the mood for a walk around the block, myself." He winked at the twins. "What do you think, girls? Shall we get a bit of air?"

Without a word, Jessica and Elizabeth followed their grandparents out of the house. On the street, Grandpa set a brisk pace. Grandma walked beside him. Elizabeth was so busy trying to keep up with them and worrying about what her parents would decide, she didn't ask any questions.

The walk seemed to go on endlessly. Finally, after two trips around the block, Grandpa led the way back into the house. Mr. and Mrs. Wakefield were sitting at the kitchen table, drinking coffee.

"Sit down," Mr. Wakefield said. Everyone joined them at the table.

Mrs. Wakefield cleared her throat. "We've

talked it over," she said, "and we think that perhaps we haven't judged the situation fairly."

Elizabeth felt a sudden surge of hope.

"We were very upset about Steven's eye," Mr. Wakefield said. "Maybe we acted without thoroughly considering the matter."

Jessica leaned forward eagerly. "Does that mean—?" she began.

Mrs. Wakefield held up her hand. "At the same time, girls, we're very disappointed that you would even consider sneaking out of the house."

Jessica bit her lip. It sounded as if they were still going to say no. Elizabeth wished that Jessica had never brought up the idea of sneaking out.

Mr. Wakefield cleared his throat. "But all things considered," he said to the twins, "we think that your grandparents are right. You should be able to go to the party. If you still want to," he added.

"If we *want* to!" Jessica cried. She jumped up and flung her arms around his neck. Then she kissed her mother. "Oh, this is wonderful!" she said, dancing around the table. "Oh, I can't wait to tell Lila!" And with that, she ran from the room, straight upstairs to the telephone.

"Thank you," Elizabeth said to her parents.

"I'm not sure that we deserve to go, after we talked about sneaking out."

Her mother smiled. "I like to think that we can trust you to remember what's right, Elizabeth."

Elizabeth turned to hug her grandparents. "And thank *you*," she said. "It's going to be a great party."

"Don't you think you'd better get ready?" Grandma asked with a little nod at the clock. "I'm sure you don't want to be late."

Elizabeth looked at the clock and gasped. The party would begin in an hour. She and Jessica would have to rush to get ready.

But when Elizabeth got upstairs, she discovered that Jessica was still on the phone to Lila. She was just finishing her story.

"So you see, Lila," she was saying, "if it hadn't been for me, we would never have gotten to go to the party."

"Hey, wait just a minute," Elizabeth interrupted. "How do you figure that? Your idea about sneaking out almost wrecked everything. I'm still surprised that Mom and Dad decided to let us go."

Jessica covered the mouthpiece of the phone with her hand. "It's simple, Lizzie," she said smoothly. "If I hadn't come up with the idea and talked to you about it where Grandma and Grandpa could hear us, they never would have known how we felt. And then they never would have stood up for us in front of Mom and Dad."

"But—" Elizabeth began.

"And without *that*," Jessica went on, "Mom and Dad wouldn't have changed their minds. So, if it hadn't been for me, we wouldn't have gotten to go." She grinned. "I think you owe me a big favor for what I've done for you. How about loaning me your new white sandals?" And without waiting to hear a word from Elizabeth, she turned back to the phone.

For a minute, Elizabeth just stared at her twin. Then she burst into laughter. Jessica always came out on top, no matter what—and always took the credit when things turned out well.

But right then, she didn't have time to worry about Jessica. She had a party to get ready for!

At last, the twins were ready. Jessica was wearing a short pink skirt with a pink-and-white striped top, and she'd borrowed Elizabeth's new white sandals. She had tied a narrow pink velvet ribbon in her hair, which hung in loose waves around her shoulders, and her little gold earrings glittered in her ears. Elizabeth was wearing a black cotton skirt, a white T-shirt, and her favorite patterned vest. Both girls were so excited at the thought of actually going to the party, they could hardly stand still.

"You two look beautiful!" Grandma exclaimed when they came down the stairs.

Grandpa gave an admiring whistle. He glanced at Grandma. "Do they remind you of anyone, Marjorie?"

"They certainly do," Grandma replied. Her eyes were warm. "You girls look exactly like your mother when she was your age!"

Grandpa broke in. "The twins are in a hurry to get to the Hangout," he said. "You can tell them all about it in the car."

Since Mr. and Mrs. Wakefield had gone to their dinner, Grandma and Grandpa were driving the twins to the party. After they had all gotten in the car and started off, Elizabeth leaned forward.

"Grandma and Grandpa," she said. "Why did you decide to stand up for us?"

Grandma and Grandpa traded glances. "Well," Grandpa said, "sometimes parents are too close to a situation to see it objectively. We thought that was what was happening in this case."

Grandma smiled. "We realized that your mom and dad were making a mistake because we remembered making a similar one with your mother."

"You mean," Jessica asked, "that you kept Mom from going somewhere?"

Grandpa reached for Grandma's hand and gave it a short squeeze. "You're thinking of when we told Alice that she couldn't go to the party at the skating rink, aren't you?" he asked.

Grandma nodded. "There had been a little trouble at the rink the month before," she explained to the twins, "and we were worried about Alice's safety. Your mother was crushed when we told her she couldn't go."

"It turned out that nothing at all happened," Grandpa said. "We were being too careful."

"And probably a bit unreasonable," Grandma added.

"And I'm sure that Alice thought we were unfair," Grandpa said quietly. "I remember how she moped around the night of the party. It was weeks before that unhappy look went out of her eyes."

Grandma turned around in her seat. "So you

see," she said, smiling at the twins, "this was a kind of second chance for us. A chance to make things right."

"And anyway," Grandpa added cheerfully, "how could we let you miss a party with Dave Carlquist?"

Jessica looked surprised. "What do you know about Dave Carlquist, Grandpa?"

"Are you kidding? I haven't listened to anybody else all week," Grandpa replied. "The radio in your room was tuned to his show, Jessica. I have to say that he's a pretty terrific deejay. And he plays interesting music, too." He grinned at Grandma. "Say, Marjorie, do you suppose it would be all right if we dropped in on the girls' party? I'd like to meet Dave Carlquist."

Jessica's eyes widened in horror at the thought of her grandparents crashing their party. "Grandpa—" she began.

Grandma laughed. "Don't worry, girls, your grandfather is teasing you!"

Elizabeth giggled. She had been a tiny bit worried herself.

Grandpa hummed a tune. Elizabeth thought she recognized it as one of Melody Power's latest singles. "Melody Power, she's a great one," he said. "And Darcy Campman, the folksinger—I really like a couple of her pieces." He began humming a different song, one of Darcy Campman's.

"I think you're surprising the twins, Charles," Grandma said.

Grandpa threw a look at Elizabeth and Jessica over his shoulder. "What's the matter?" he demanded. "What did you think your grandparents listened to on the radio? Moldy oldies?"

And with that, the four of them burst into laughter.

Ten

◇

Music was playing loudly and the Hangout's dance floor was already filled when Elizabeth and Jessica arrived. On a small stage, Dave Carlquist sat at a console, behind a microphone. He was wearing earphones and playing records.

"Oh, Lizzie," Jessica said happily. "Isn't it terrific? Aren't you glad I was able to fix it so we could come?"

"Actually," Elizabeth said, "I really don't think *you* were the one who fixed it so we could come. I think Grandma and Grandpa did."

Jessica ignored her sister. "Look, there's Lila!" she exclaimed. "I've got to go talk to her." She walked off in the direction of a group of Unicorns.

"Elizabeth!" Amy exclaimed, coming up behind her. "I can't believe you're here. How did you manage to change your parents' minds?"

Elizabeth laughed. "I'll tell you all about it," she promised. "But first, why don't we go up to the stage and say hello to Dave Carlquist?"

"Jessica!" Ellen cried in disbelief. "I couldn't believe it when Lila said you were going to be here. How did you get out?" She lowered her voice. "Did you *sneak* out?"

"Well," Jessica began. "First I told Elizabeth there was no way—"

"Jessica, isn't that your sister up there?" Lila interrupted.

"Where?" Jessica turned around.

"Up there, talking to Dave Carlquist!" Tamara Chase said. She squealed as Dave put his arm around Elizabeth's shoulders and gave her a quick squeeze. "Does she *know* him?"

"We—" Jessica began.

"I remember!" Mary Wallace exclaimed. "Elizabeth won the contest to name Dave Carlquist's show, didn't she?"

Jessica frowned. Were the Unicorns going to

stand around all night and talk about Elizabeth? "Come on," she said to Lila impatiently, "let's go get something to eat."

Tamara turned to Mary. "Maybe if we ask Elizabeth, she could get Dave to play that song we've been wanting to hear," she said.

"I bet she could," Mary said. "Let's go ask." Tamara and Mary headed toward the stage without even so much as a goodbye. Ellen watched them go.

"I'm starved," Jessica said. "Aren't you hungry, Ellen?"

"A little," Ellen admitted. "But I have a song I've been dying to hear. Maybe Elizabeth will ask Dave to play it—and dedicate it to *me*." She hurried after Tamara and Mary.

Jessica made a face. "Who cares about a song being dedicated to her?" she said to Lila.

A moment later, Jessica could see Mary, Tamara, and Ellen motion to Elizabeth to come over to the edge of the stage. They chatted for a minute or two. Then Elizabeth went back to talk to Dave Carlquist, and a moment or two later, he turned on his mike.

"That was one of my personal favorites, Melody Power's hit, 'Happy to Be With You,'" he said. "Now I want to play a request from Elizabeth Wakefield. You may remember that Elizabeth is the one who came up with the name of my show, 'The Awesome Hour.' "

Jessica saw that everybody was looking at Elizabeth, who was grinning. Jessica was beginning to feel very irritated.

"The next song," Dave Carlquist said, "is Johnny Buck's newest and hottest number, called 'Taking the Cake.' Elizabeth wants me to play it for someone who really *does* take the cake. Her twin, Jessica Wakefield!"

Everybody turned to look at Jessica. After an instant's surprise, she smiled and waved. Maybe she wasn't that upset after all.

"Hi, Jessica."

Jessica turned. It was Todd Wilkins, and he was grinning.

"I thought maybe you'd like to dance. I mean, since this is your song."

Jessica nodded happily, aware that Lila's envious glance was now fixed on *her*. Todd led her out onto the dance floor. Johnny Buck's music had a strong, fast beat that made her feet want to move. Jessica knew she was a terrific dancer, and Todd wasn't too bad either.

After their dance, Todd thanked her. As soon as he had stepped back into the crowd, Lila, Ellen, and Mary rushed up to Jessica. Caroline Pearce, Jessica saw with great satisfaction, wasn't far behind them.

"How romantic," Ellen gushed. "Jessica, you and Todd Wilkins are meant for each other."

"Todd does seem a bit interested in you, Jessica," Lila admitted.

"Do you think he wants to be your boyfriend?" Mary asked. "That would be so cool!"

"Maybe," Jessica said with a mysterious smile. "And maybe not."

"Jessica," Caroline asked, "I just *have* to know what's going on with you and Todd. I want to mention the two of you in my gossip column."

"Todd and I just danced together, that's all," Jessica said calmly. She gave an unconcerned laugh. "It's no big deal."

"I think," Mary spoke up, "Todd has a crush on Jessica."

"Can I quote you on that?" Caroline asked.

"Sure," Mary said happily.

Caroline turned to Jessica. "And how do you feel about Todd, Jessica?"

Jessica smiled. "It's a secret."

Caroline laughed. "Jessica," she said admiringly, "you are so cool."

Jessica laughed, but inside, she wasn't cool at all. She was jubilant. None of her friends had ever had a real boyfriend before. If she became Todd's girlfriend, it would be a first. She would be a celebrity.

The party was almost over. Elizabeth and Amy said goodbye to Dave Carlquist, and thanked Aaron and his parents for a terrific evening. Elizabeth was looking around for Jessica when Caroline Pearce strolled up to her.

"Well, Elizabeth," Caroline said, "what do you think? For the record," she added.

"Think about what?" Elizabeth wanted to know.

"What do you think about the new couple?" Caroline said. "I'm getting reactions for my gossip column."

Elizabeth was confused. "The new couple?" she asked.

Caroline's eyebrows shot up. "Don't you know? Jessica and Todd Wilkins, of *course*."

"Oh," Elizabeth said.

"You mean," Caroline asked unbelievingly, "you didn't know? They've been dancing together all night."

Amy gave a short laugh. "They danced together *once*. What's the big deal?"

"Amy, you are *so* naive," Caroline said in a scornful voice. She flounced off.

"How ridiculous," Amy said.

"Ridiculous," Elizabeth repeated.

Amy looked thoughtful. "But you know Caroline," she said. "In a day or two, it'll be all over Sweet Valley that Jessica and Todd are a couple."

Elizabeth had a feeling that Amy was right.

"What's going on with you and Todd Wilkins?" Elizabeth asked Jessica, when they were getting ready for bed.

Jessica looked up from brushing her hair. There was a dreamy look in her eyes. "Did you see us dancing together? Isn't he a *great* dancer?"

"I didn't see you, but I think everybody else did." Elizabeth paused. "Especially Caroline Pearce," she added. "She told me that you and Todd are a couple."

Jessica smiled. "Did she?" she asked lightly. "I wonder where she got that idea?"

Elizabeth wondered what was really going on inside Jessica's head. "Jessica, do you . . . do you *like* Todd?" she asked carefully.

"That's what Caroline wanted to know, too," Jessica replied.

"And what did you say?"

"I said it was a secret," Jessica said. And even though Elizabeth tried to get her to talk, that was Jessica's last word on the subject.

The next morning at breakfast, everyone was quiet. The twins were sleepy from staying up so late the night before. Everyone knew that Grandma and Grandpa were leaving that evening. Elizabeth felt a little sad.

"I wish you two didn't have to leave so soon," Mrs. Wakefield said.

"It would be nice if we could stay," Grandma said with a smile. She handed the plate of pancakes to Steven, who quickly helped himself to half of them. "But we promised your sister that we'd come and see their new house in San Diego."

"I wish Liz and I could go with you," Jessica

said. "I'd love to see Robin. It's been *such* a long time since we've been together." She threw a quick glance at her parents to see if they had taken the hint.

"Not now, Jessica," Mrs. Wakefield responded automatically.

Jessica pounced. "You mean, we can go some other time?"

"We'll see," her father said. "Well, what would you two like to do on your last day in Sweet Valley?"

"Do?" Grandpa asked vaguely. He scratched his head with a puzzled look. "Marjorie, was there something I was supposed to do today?"

"The tickets, Charles," Grandma reminded him. "You were supposed to see about the tickets."

Grandpa smacked the side of his head. "The tickets!" he exclaimed. "Of course! I must be getting old. I'd forgotten all about them."

"What tickets, Grandpa?" Elizabeth asked.

Grandpa patted his pockets, one after another. "I wish I could remember where I put them," he said.

"What tickets is he looking for?" Jessica asked Grandma.

Grandma put a finger to her lips. "Shh," she

said. "Don't distract your grandfather when he's looking for something."

Grandpa was searching frantically through his wallet. "You don't suppose I lost them, do you?"

"If you'd tell us what tickets you're looking for, Grandpa," Jessica said, "we might be able to help you find them."

"Tickets?" Grandpa asked, frowning. "Tickets?" Then his expression suddenly cleared. "Oh, yes, of course! Now I remember where I put them." And with a wide grin, he reached over the table and passed his hand beside Jessica's head. When he pulled his hand back, there were five yellow tickets in it.

"Oh, Grandpa," Jessica said good-naturedly, "you had them up your sleeve all the time."

Steven laughed loudly. "Boy, he sure got *you*, Jessica. The oldest trick in the world, and you fell for it like a ton of bricks."

Jessica gave Steven a dirty look. "I knew where they were. I was just going along with the joke." She smiled coyly as she turned back to her grandfather and said, "What are the tickets for, Grandpa?"

Grandpa frowned. "I don't think I exactly remember," he said. He adjusted his glasses on his nose and held the tickets out to read them, while everybody watched. "D-A-R-C-Y," he spelled out slowly. "C-A-M-P-M-A-N. Dar-cy Camp-man."

"Darcy Campman!" Jessica yelled. "Grandpa, *really*?"

Grandpa looked up. "Yes, that's right. That's exactly what they are. Tickets to the Darcy Campman benefit concert this afternoon. Practically front-row seats, too."

Steven looked stunned. "*You* bought tickets to the Darcy Campman Benefit?"

Grandpa nodded. "Your grandmother and I have been planning to go all week. It was really tough to get tickets, and they told me that five was the smallest number I could buy." He shook his head. "I was supposed to find three people to take these other tickets, but I forgot. Now how in the world am I going to find anybody to go with your grandmother and me at *this* late hour!"

Elizabeth smiled. She knew that Grandpa was just teasing them. He and Grandma had planned this all along.

Steven cleared his throat. "Grandpa, I think I could fit it into my schedule."

Jessica was practically jumping up and down. "I'll go, Grandpa! I'll go!" she announced.

Grandpa smiled at Jessica. "You mean you

wouldn't be too embarrassed to let your friends see you with a couple of old fogeys?''

Jessica shook her head. "Not at the Darcy Campman Benefit!'' she said.

Elizabeth smiled. "I'd love to go, too, Grandpa.''

"Whew,'' Grandpa said, with an exaggerated whistle of relief. "I thought for a minute there that Grandma and I would have to sit in a row with three empty seats beside us! You kids saved my life!''

That afternoon, Jessica, Elizabeth, Steven, and their grandparents went to the Darcy Campman Benefit. Darcy Campman was so close that Elizabeth and Jessica could almost believe that she was singing just to them.

And once, when Elizabeth unexpectedly heard Grandpa humming along to the music, she leaned over and gave him a big hug. What a terrific surprise this had turned out to be. She had thought that her grandparents wouldn't be able to do anything exciting, but she was happy to have been wrong.

"We've had an absolutely marvelous time,'' Grandma said, as they all stood together in the airport. People around them were hurrying to get on the plane for San Diego.

"That's right," Grandpa said, with a warm smile for Elizabeth. "It's been great to have somebody who'll go jogging with me." He grinned at Jessica. "And somebody who doesn't mind having a trick or two played on her," he added mischievously.

"Tell Robin we want to see her as soon as Mom and Dad say we can come," Jessica said.

"We will," Grandma promised. "And we want you to come and visit us in Florida."

They gave everyone another hug and kiss. Then they were gone.

"I'm so glad they came," Jessica said as the family walked back to the car. "I'm going to miss them."

"Even though you finally get your room back?" her mother teased.

"Elizabeth's probably the one who'll be glad about that," Jessica replied, with a knowing glance at her sister.

"You're right," Elizabeth said. But she knew that she would miss her grandparents, too. It had been such a great visit. "I wish they didn't have to leave," she said.

"I wish we could have gone with them," Jessica said with a sigh. "I really want to see Robin."

Elizabeth nodded. "That would be terrific, wouldn't it?" she asked.

"Especially if we could go alone," Jessica whispered to Elizabeth.

Will Jessica and Elizabeth get to go to San Diego to see their cousin, Robin? Find out in Sweet Valley Twins #42, **Jessica's Secret.**

SWEET VALLEY TWINS™

COULD *YOU* BE THE NEXT SWEET VALLEY READER OF THE MONTH?

ENTER BANTAM BOOKS' SWEET VALLEY CONTEST & SWEEPSTAKES IN ONE!

Calling all Sweet Valley Fans! Here's a chance to appear in a Sweet Valley book!

We know how important Sweet Valley is to you. That's why we've come up with a Sweet Valley celebration offering exciting opportunities to have YOUR thoughts printed in a Sweet Valley book!

"How do I become a Sweet Valley Reader of the Month?"

It's easy. Just write a one-page essay (no more than 150 words, please) telling us a little about yourself, and why you like to read Sweet Valley books. We will pick the best essays and print them along with the winner's photo in the back of upcoming Sweet Valley books. Every month there will be a new Sweet Valley Twins Reader of the Month!

And, there's more!

Just sending in your essay makes you eligible for the Grand Prize drawing for a trip to Los Angeles, California! This once-in-a-life-time trip includes round-trip airfare, accommodations for 5 nights (economy double occupancy), a rental car, and meal allowance. (Approximate retail value: $4,500.)

Don't wait! Write your essay today.
No purchase necessary. See the next page for Official rules.

AN 143 SVT

ENTER BANTAM BOOKS' SWEET VALLEY READER OF THE MONTH SWEEPSTAKES

OFFICIAL RULES:

READER OF THE MONTH ESSAY CONTEST

1. No Purchase Is Necessary. Enter by hand printing your name, address, date of birth and telephone number on a plain 3" x 5" card, and sending this card along with your essay telling us about yourself and why you like to read Sweet Valley books to:

READER OF THE MONTH
SWEET VALLEY TWINS
BANTAM BOOKS
YR MARKETING
666 FIFTH AVENUE
NEW YORK, NEW YORK 10103

2. Reader of the Month Contest Winner. For each month from June 1, 1990 through December 31, 1990, a Sweet Valley Twins Reader of the Month will be chosen from the entries received during that month. The winners will have their essay and photo published in the back of an upcoming Sweet Valley Twins title.

3. Enter as often as you wish, but each essay must be original and each entry must be mailed in a separate envelope bearing sufficient postage. All completed entries must be postmarked and received by Bantam no later than December 31, 1990, in order to be eligible for the Essay Contest and Sweepstakes. Entrants must be between the ages of 6 and 16 years old. Each essay must be no more than 150 words and must be typed double-spaced or neatly printed on one side of an 8 1/2" x 11" page which has the entrant's name, address, date of birth and telephone number at the top. The essays submitted will be judged each month by Bantam's Marketing Department on the basis of originality, creativity, thoughtfulness, and writing ability, and all of Bantam's decisions are final and binding. Essays become the property of Bantam Books and none will be returned. Bantam reserves the right to edit the winning essays for length and readability. Essay Contest winners will be notified by mail within 30 days of being chosen. In the event there are an insufficient number of essays received in any month which meet the minimum standards established by the judges, Bantam reserves the right not to choose a Reader of the Month. Winners have 30 days from the date of Bantam's notice in which to respond, or an alternate Reader of the Month winner will be chosen. Bantam is not responsible for incomplete or lost or misdirected entries.

4. Winners of the Essay Contest and their parents or legal guardians may be required to execute an Affidavit of Eligibility and Promotional Release supplied by Bantam. Entering the Reader of the Month Contest constitutes permission for use of the winner's name, address, likeness and contest submission for publicity and promotional purposes, with no additional compensation.

5. Employees of Bantam Books, Bantam Doubleday Dell Publishing Group, Inc., and their subsidiaries and affiliates, and their immediate family members are not eligible to enter the Essay Contest. The Essay Contest is open to residents of the U.S. and Canada (excluding the province of Quebec), and is void wherever prohibited or restricted by law. All applicable federal, state, and local regulations apply.

READER OF THE MONTH SWEEPSTAKES

6. Sweepstakes Entry. No purchase is necessary. Every entrant in the Sweet Valley High, Sweet Valley Twins and Sweet Valley Kids Essay Contest whose completed entry is received by December 31, 1990 will be entered in the Reader of the Month Sweepstakes. The Grand Prize winner will be selected in a random drawing from all completed entries received on or about February 1, 1991 and will be notified by mail. Bantam's decision is final and binding. Odds of winning are dependent on the number of entries received. The prize is non-transferable and no substitution is allowed. The Grand Prize winner must be accompanied on the trip by a parent or legal guardian. Taxes are the sole responsibility of the prize winner. Trip must be taken within one year of notification and is subject to availability. Travel arrangements will be made for the winner and, once made, no changes will be allowed.

7. 1 Grand Prize. A six day, five night trip for two to Los Angeles, California. Includes round-trip coach airfare, accommodations for 5 nights (economy double occupancy), a rental car — economy model, and spending allowance for meals. (Approximate retail value: $4,500.)

8. The Grand Prize winner and their parent or legal guardian may be required to execute an Affidavit of Eligibility and Promotional Release supplied by Bantam. Entering the Reader of the Month Sweepstakes constitutes permission for use of the winner's name, address, and the likeness for publicity and promotional purposes, with no additional compensation.

9. Employees of Bantam Books, Bantam Doubleday Dell Publishing Group, Inc., and their subsidiaries and affiliates, and their immediate family members are not eligible to enter this Sweepstakes. The Sweepstakes is open to residents of the U.S. and Canada (excluding the province of Quebec), and is void wherever prohibited or restricted by law. If a Canadian resident, the Grand Prize winner will be required to correctly answer an arithmetical skill-testing question in order to receive the prize. All applicable federal, state, and local regulations apply. The Grand Prize will be awarded in the name of the minor's parent or guardian. Taxes, if any, are the winner's sole responsibility.

10. For the name of the Grand Prize winner and the names of the winners of the Sweet Valley High, Sweet Valley Twins and Sweet Valley Kids Essay Contests, send a stamped, self-addressed envelope entirely separate from your entry to: Bantam Books, Sweet Valley Reader of the Month Winners, Young Readers Marketing, 666 Fifth Avenue, New York, New York 10103. The winners list will be available after April 15, 1991.